HIS BLOOD BROTHER'S LIFE

Egil's warning came too late. A pair of soldiers dropped from a low place on the bluff, hoping to kill them quickly. Karne was much lighter than his opponent, weakened by blood loss and shock. He'd never had Egil's hand-to-hand skills. Swiftly Egil killed his own attacker. With relief he saw Karne's opponent sinking to the ground, an amazed look on his face, trying to push his intestines back inside his belly.

But Karne himself was sinking against the bluff wall, also wounded in the abdomen. Dark blood streamed from his shoulder and chest. Egil sprinted to the radio, dialing the emergency frequency. His closest friend was bleeding to death. . . .

WINTER WORLD
Egil's Book

WINTER WORLD

EGIL'S BOOK
C.J. MILLS

ACE BOOKS, NEW YORK

For the Spring 1988 creative writing classes at Coon
Rapids (Minn.) Senior High School,
in appreciation for help given.

This book is an Ace original edition,
and has never been previously published.

EGIL'S BOOK

An Ace Book / published by arrangement with
the author

PRINTING HISTORY
Ace edition / February 1991

ISBN: 0-441-89444-5

Ace Books are published by The Berkley Publishing Group,
200 Madison Avenue, New York, New York 10016.
The name "ACE" and the "A" logo
are trademarks belonging to Charter Communications, Inc.

PRINTED IN THE UNITED STATES OF AMERICA

10 9 8 7 6 5 4 3 2 1

PROLOGUE

Starker IV's round World Council chamber flowed with color. Freemen in brilliant sarks and hosen, men of the noble Houses in rich fabrics and glittering jewels, Council guards in red uniforms, all talked and laughed and renewed old friendships and old enmities after the winter's confinement. But there was apprehension in the air as well as the excitement of Thawtime. Everyone had been waiting since the Frosttime Council for the results of the Patrol's investigation into the attempted assassinations against Karne Halarek, Heir in House Halarek, aboard the Gildship *Aldefara*. Everyone knew the ship had left its orbit around Starker IV only days before. That meant the trial was finally over, sentences handed out to any Federation citizens involved, and conclusions about Starker IV citizen involvement reached. Soon Gild representatives would bring the conclusions to Council.

There lay a great deal of the apprehension. The necessity of a trial had required the Gild to leave the *Aldefara* in orbit around Starker IV from Uhl until Verdain, more than half a year Starker time. A ship idle, its crew drawing onerous-duty pay (there could be no shore leave except at Gildport), its passengers also detained and very unhappy about the long confinement, the expense of bringing the captain's peers from halfway across the galaxy to be his jury— no, the Gild was not happy. Much worse, someone had violated the Gild's sacred neutrality by taking feud aboard the Gildship. No one, ever, took feud aboard a Gildship. Yet someone had, and the Gild had lost three passengers in the attempts to kill Karne Halarek. Many men present believed House Harlan had been behind the assassination attempts. If it had, House Harlan had put Starker IV's connection with the rest of the galaxy at risk.

Karne Halarek sat inside a clear-sided protective box, confined for his own protection by the old Council chairman. Karne ran a hand through his hair, chewed his lower lip, and looked out at the semicircle of prep tables of the Nine Families. His unusual golden eyes fixed on an empty chair across the semicircle, the chair behind the Harlan prep table where Richard, duke-designate, would soon sit.

Across a broad aisle from the Harlan benches, Freemen filed into their seats. The tiers belonging to the minor Houses, on Halarek's left beyond another broad aisle, were already almost full. A blat of horns and the clashing together of the Council soldiers' ceremonial swords and pikes announced the arrival of the new Council chairman. The chamber's main doors opened and the Marquis of Gormsby marched importantly to the chairman's desk, set in the open center of the chamber.

Karne Halarek's eyes narrowed, all the emotion he could allow to show. Two years of a Council under the hand of a Harlan ally. Karne's eyes flicked over the brightly colored ranks of Freemen. They would never interfere in what they considered the business of the Houses and feud was definitely the business of the Houses. Karne summoned all the control he had learned at the Academy. He would need all the skills he had learned there to keep this political situation from turning into a military one—again. Karne felt again the old rush of anger at his sire. Trev Halarek had been so sure at least one of his sons other than Karne would survive that he had sent Karne off to Altair. Well, Trev and Jerem and Kerel and Liam had been dead a year and House Halarek had to depend on Karne's abilities now. If he did not leave this meeting head-of-House, Halarek would be leaderless and would die as Council, under Richard Harlan's control, tore it apart as vassalage and smallholdings for the Nine.

Richard Harlan walked purposefully to his place at the center of his prep table, brushing past the Family men who rose from the back benches or stood in the aisle or waved eager arms for his attention. Richard rested his fingertips on the table's polished surface and leaned on them. The look he sent Karne raised an angry murmur from the men on the Halarek benches.

The Larga Alysha Halarek rose to speak. Karne felt admiration for her courage in standing to speak to Council, knowing how strong their enemies were and how little chance a woman, even a woman who was regent in her House, would have of being heard. Karne smothered the rush of anger that followed. He should be beside her at the table to support her efforts on his behalf!

"Alysha Halarek, Larga and regent in Halarek," she said, identifying herself as was required. "Since the new chairman"—she gave Gormsby a curt nod of recognition—"has decided that the matter of the Harlan trusteeship is more important than the Gild report that may implicate House Harlan in treasonous acts, Council must know this: House Harlan and its trustee laid siege to our manor three days earlier than the law allows."

Her statement brought a gasp of surprise from those who did not know what had happened.

"Their ships—"

The chairman rapped his gavel on his desk. "Women do not speak here, milady. And Richard Harlan was already standing."

The Larga stiffened. "Only because he had not yet sat down, milord. Richard may not speak for Harlan now, anyway. Kingsland, the Harlan trustee, speaks for Harlan."

"Unfortunately, milady," the chairman said smoothly, "your House has no male representative here and that means your House has no official voice."

"Council accepted Trev's wish that I be appointed regent."

Gormsby nodded and smiled unpleasantly. "So it did, milady. I recognize Harlan."

Karne sprang to his feet, ready to shout his indignation and anger, then collected himself and forced himself to speak in a level voice. "I am Lharr in Halarek in all but name. If the Larga may not speak, it is *my* right."

"You are not yet of age and I've already recognized Harlan," the chairman said, and turned his head away from the Halarek side of the room.

Members of Council murmured angrily. A man from one of the minor Houses stood and shook his fist at the chairman. A cluster of Freemen rose and walked to the aisle around the back of the room, where they conferred quietly.

Richard began speaking, long before the angry murmuring died down enough that Karne could hear what he was saying. " . . . most important of these is the continuing humiliation of being governed for as if I were a minor." Richard looked pointedly at Karne. "It embarrasses my House to be punished for one entire winter on such a small offense—"

"Small offense!" the lord of House McNeece roared, bounding to his feet. "You laid siege without notice. The forty-day law is all that keeps the wolves among the Nine from eating up small Houses like mine!"

"I have the floor, Van," Richard cut in smoothly. "You'll get your turn to speak." Richard turned again toward the chairman. "As I was saying, the sentence humiliated my House and thereby lessened my credibility with my vassals. The previous chairman added to this the disgrace of compelling my trustee to withdraw my forces from the site of a lawful siege."

"The lawfulness of that siege has been questioned, Lord Richard," Lord Gormsby put in, his tone indicating doubts about McNeece's motives for interrupting.

Richard bowed to indicate he had heard. "I gave the required public notice." He turned toward the half-circle of Families. "Noble Houses, consider also that the charges laid against my House at the last Council by the minor, Karne Halarek, and his regent, caused the paralysis, eventual insanity, and death of the noble Asten Harlan, my sire.

My House has suffered enough, lords and Freemen, at the hands of this foreign-bred, foreign-trained incompetent, Karne Halarek. Give me the reins, let me rule my House as was my sire's wish!" Richard slammed his palm against the tabletop for emphasis.

Karne burned inside, but he let nothing show. Concealed in Harlan's last words was the common knowledge that Trev Halarek had never wanted his slender, wiry third son to rule. In all his seventeen winters, Karne had not gotten used to that contempt. He did not think he ever would.

You misjudge me, Richard, if you expect to taunt me with such remarks. I've lived with them too long.

Gormsby called for a vote, despite protests from the Nine and even from the Freemen. Bailiffs began distributing ballots amid much angry whispering, overloud rustling of papers, and much coughing and shifting in seats. The next moment, the chamber boomed with furious pounding on the main doors. Men from the back benches of von Schuss and deVree forced their way through the throng of observers clogging the back aisle and shoved the doors unceremoniously open. Everyone turned to look. What they saw were soldiers in Council red pushing a delegation of Gild First Merchants away from the doors. This was the expected delegation from the most powerful trade group in the galaxy and Council soldiers were pushing them away.

"My lord of Gormsby, what does this mean?" the Earl of Justin roared.

"Aye, tell us!" The angry chorus shook the gallery floor until it rattled.

Baron von Schuss rose, his usually florid face almost purple with anger. Other heads-of House rose, many of them clamoring for attention. Gormsby glanced toward Richard Harlan, who looked away, then toward Garren Odonnel, newly Lharr in Odonnel, who shrugged. Gormsby licked his lips with a dart of his tongue.

"Why, my lords, why, I—I have no idea what's happening. Bring those men in."

Von Schuss and deVree escorted the ruffled Gild officers to the space in front of the chairman's desk, then they stepped back behind their tables. The First Merchants brushed their rumpled uniforms into order with quick, short strokes. The room had become so quiet everyone could hear the rough sound of hands against stiff fabric. A gray-haired Terran at the center of the group faced the semicircle of the Nine.

"Lords of the Nine Families, I, John Gaunt of Gild Central, say to you that I have nowhere been treated so badly in my entire career, and I've dealt with the barbarians of Joren and the cannibals of Sabo! If the matter before you were not of great urgency, I would take my delegation back to Gildport and then Gild Central and recommend that Starker IV be made off-limits to Gildships for an indefinite time!"

Lords and Freemen alike gasped at the idea of such a disaster.

Gaunt went on, his voice shaking with anger, to describe the great expense to the Gild of the investigation and trial. Gormsby's eyes darted here and there to his allies on the Council.

Two years of this. Can my House survive two years of this kind of partisanship? Karne tried to think what House would take the chairmanship in two years and realized this was yet another hole in what he should know about his world's politics and did not. He again cursed Trev Halarek's confidence that he would continue to outwit Asten Harlan as he had for twenty years. Well, he had outwitted Asten, but not Richard.

Today it was not just the survival of House Halarek at stake. Egil might yet be alive and Egil was the son of a great freemerchant on Balder. Surely the Gild would help Egil stay out of Council hands. *That* couldn't damage the Gild's absolute neutrality, could it? Egil had stayed behind at the guardpost on the edge of Zinn and—even with hands frozen solid—kept the Runners at bay so Karne could escape to tell Council of the illegal siege. Now Karne was under Council arrest, Richard was free and, Council claimed, Egil had disappeared. Egil might yet be alive, but Karne was quite sure Gormsby would not help find him. Well, the Gild was here, and very angry, and the Council would not risk angering the Gild more. Perhaps Gild medics could even save Egil's hands.

I may or may not be able to save my House, Karne thought, *but I can by-the-Guardians try to save Egil.*

The thought gave Karne new energy. He shoved open the door of the plastic box, pushed aside the Council soldiers and Halarek cousins who leaped up to stop him, and strode to John Gaunt's side. Gaunt stopped speaking and stared at him coldly.

Karne refused to let the man's intimidating look stop him. He lightly touched head and heart in the Federation gesture of respect. "Gentlehom, I interrupt you for the sake of a man's life. He needs the Gild's medical attention at once."

The Gildsman looked Karne up and down. "And who be you?"

"Karne Halarek, gentlehom. Please, send men for my friend, Egil Olafsson, before you continue your report. He stayed at Council Guardpost 105 to protect me from the Runners. His hands had been frozen solid, gentlehom. Your med officers can perhaps save them, or at least save his life."

"Olafsson claims to be Halarek's brother," Garren Odonnel sneered.

Thoughts flitted like shadows across the Gildsman's face. "If he's your brother, there's nothing I can do for him. The Nine were told in Uhl that because of the—events—aboard the *Aldefara*, the Gild will carry no passengers from the Families anywhere."

Karne stiffened. "My enemies would hurt me through my friend, gentlehom, and I suspect Egil is in their—Council's—custody. Council supposedly sent a medical team right after—right after my arrest." He kept his voice quiet and reasonable, though he was shaking with rage at Odonnel's attempt to prevent Egil from getting help. "The Gild is a neutral presence here, gentlehom, and Egil is a citizen of Balder, the son of freemerchant Odin Olafsson, who—"

Gaunt's face lighted with recognition. He turned and

spoke rapidly and quietly to a companion, who ran from the chamber. Gaunt turned to Karne again.

"First Merchant Ronoke goes to prepare our shuttle. Your friend will be taken to our ship the minute your Council turns him over to us."

Karne bowed deeply. "I'll always be grateful to you, gentlehom. Egil Olafsson is closer than kin to me."

"How will we know the chairman has given us the right man, young sir?"

Karne felt glad for the first time in weeks. He grinned at Gaunt. "He's the image of his father, gentlehom."

Gaunt grinned back, then sobered and turned to Chairman Gormsby. "You will release this young man to us immediately, on pain of Gild embargo."

Gormsby licked his lips and looked at Odonnel and Harlan. Odonnel doodled with his stylus on the tabletop. Harlan looked at the ceiling.

"We of the Gharr always deal honorably with the Gild, First Merchant."

Gaunt looked down his nose at the marquis, plainly disbelieving, and pointedly turned away. Gormsby flushed and licked his lips again. Gaunt spoke, more to the Council than to the chairman.

"You will regret for years anything but the immediate release of this young man, Council of Starker IV. He comes from a great merchant family and a powerful ally of the Gild."

Gormsby cleared his throat and fumbled through the papers on his desk, sent for a Council medical officer, conferred, fumbled through the papers again. "A med team was sent to care for him as soon as the call came through, First Merchant, but we—we do not have the young man."

Karne went rigid. Was the man lying?

Gaunt turned slowly, his eyes and face hard. "Then who does?"

Gormsby shuffled through the papers again, looked up, looked away. "The—ah—the rescue party found no one at Post 105, First Merchant. The place had been ransacked, destroyed almost. There were no medical supplies left, no food, or clothing, or blankets, or weapons. And no Olafsson. The Runners seem to have taken him, First Merchant."

Karne saw only blackness for a moment. Egil gone. No Egil, ever again. No one the Runners took ever came back. Shock and then grief tore through Karne.

Everyone I love dies here. First Jerem, who should have been Lharr, then Kerel and Liam and now Egil!

Karne took deep, gulping breaths and summoned all his training to control his grief. He had to put his grief to one side right now. He did so, but only with great difficulty. He would have to mourn Egil later. This was a moment of great danger, for Egil and for Halarek. Harlan could not help but know the high value Karne placed on the huge blond Balderman and if Harlan, or Council for Harlan, were in truth holding him and not Runners . . .

Gaunt was speaking again, the report this time, describing the murder attempts aboard the *Aldefara* and the trial verdict that the captain of the ship had acted at the instigation of and as agent for Asten Harlan. The captain had lost his captain's papers and been sentenced to ten years at hard labor in the mines of Arhash. Gaunt dropped photos of the evidence on the desk of Freeman Gashen of the freecity of Neeran, then folded his own papers over with a snap. "Lords and Freemen of the Gharr, the Gild has acted to the limits of its codes and charters. However, I have also left with Frem Gashen Gild satellite pix of House Harlan flitters in Zinn, pix taken twenty to twenty-one Narn of last year. The Gild leaves these as information only and not as an interference in Gharr politics."

Gaunt and his delegation filed out, the sounds of their going buried beneath the roar of shock and outrage that swept the chamber.

Apparently some hadn't believed Harlan flitters shot mine down over Zinn, Karne told himself. Unmarked flitters. Gang assassination. Both serious infractions of the laws of feud.

Men of the Nine shouted at clan enemies. Freemen pointed fingers and shouted accusations at some of the Nine. Men of the minor Houses, some even standing on their benches, roared for recognition by the chairman. Others melted into the ranks of the Freemen, causing eddies of color and noise.

Chairman Gormsby pounded his gavel and cried, "Lords of Starker IV, Freemen, minor Houses, order! Order, please! Lords and Freemen!"

No one paid attention. When the noise began to fade a little, Karne strode to the center of the open space in front of the chairman's chair. He raised his uninjured arm for quiet. Slowly, starting with House Halarek and spreading to its allies and then the minor Houses, the noise abated. Karne did not face the chairman, as custom required, but spoke to the semicircle of Families and to the tiers of Freemen on the Families' left.

"My lords, a jury declared that the attempts on my life aboard the *Aldefara* were the work of Asten Harlan. The Gild brought the report and the Gild has always been scrupulously honest. Does anyone here doubt the word of the Gild?"

No one said a word. No one dared. The Gild was already angry enough to pull out.

Karne waited for his point to sink in, then continued. "I say, accept the Gild's report and the starship captain's conviction as grounds to continue the Harlan trusteeship indefinitely. If these are not enough, there"—he pointed to Gashen's desk—"are pix that support the claim I made at the Frosttime Council that Harlan assassins attacked me and my escorts in Zinn."

Richard Harlan slammed the Harlan table with his open hand. "The attack in Zinn was my sire's act. What do my sire's acts have to do with me? Nothing! Nothing at all! I won't listen to an enemy of my clan plot its destruction!"

Karne pointed a finger at Harlan and, despite his willing, the finger trembled. "*You* were there in Zinn. *You* set siege too early."

"I gave the notice required by law."

"Aye, that you did." Karne laughed, a grim, frozen sound. "The whole planet heard you. But thirty-seven days after that, only my House heard your transports landing."

"You lie!" Richard Harlan leaned over his table, his face reddening with anger.

"I tell the truth!" Karne spun away from Harlan and fixed each of the lords of the remaining Nine with his eyes. "I have Gild pix to support what I said, both about the siege and about the attack in Zinn. House Harlan thinks itself above our laws. That's very dangerous for all of us, not just Halarek. Vote now to continue the trusteeship!"

Gormsby rapped his gavel and shouted. "I'm in charge here!"

Derisive catcalls and cries of "Are you?" came from the back benches of von Schuss and Justin.

"I say when we vote," the chairman continued stubbornly.

"The vote! The vote now!" cried many voices among the minor Houses.

"I gave the notice required by law," Richard Harlan shouted above the noise. "Give me my rightful heritage!"

Unexpectedly, many voices in the Freemen's section objected violently to this.

"Stay out of Family business!" Richard roared at them.

"The laying of siege, the breaking of Council law, *is* Freemen's business. It's the *world's* business." Hareem Gashen stood before the Freemen's speaking station, waving the Gild pix.

Karne vaulted onto the Halarek prep table. "The Nine have their laws." His voice carried above the rest. "They're harsh, but we've always obeyed them. Now one of us wants exemption. If Council grants Harlan exemption from our law by lifting the trusteeship, no one will be safe."

"Exemption!" Harlan snarled. "I'll 'exempt' you, Halarek."

Suddenly Richard had a knife. Karne watched, frozen by the unreality of a weapon in Council. No one brought weapons into Council. The knife left Harlan's hand and flew toward him. Death, in the Council chamber, before he had reached any of his goals for himself or for his House. The knife tumbled toward him. Karne wanted to move but seemed to have lost the power.

Someone rammed into him from the side, though no one
had been there before. The knife skimmed past Karne's ear
and sank into something with a *thunk*. There was a little
sigh and the weight that had pushed him slid down his back
and right arm. It caught for a moment in his sling, then settled against the back of his legs. Karne glanced down. The
Larga's body slumped across the prep table, blood oozing
slowly around the knife protruding from her side.

Karne dropped to his knees and felt for a pulse. *Not her.
Guardians! Not Mother!*

There was no pulse. A Council medical officer crouched
beside him, pushed him courteously aside, felt the Larga's
pulse, pulled out the knife, looked at Karne.

"She's dead, milord. I'm sorry." He spoke softly, apolo-
getically. "I'll call people to prepare her for the trip home."
His hand settled briefly on Karne's shoulder in comfort,
then he rose and went away.

Jerem, Kerel, Liam, Egil, now the Larga. All dead.

Karne raised his head. The room swam in a red haze with
only Richard clear. Three Harlan men were wrestling with
him, trying to get a stunner out of his hand. Harlan. Harlan
expected exemption from the laws against off-world attacks,
against gang assassination, against laying siege early. With
Gormsby as chairman, Harlan would probably *get* exemption. Even after this.

Karne sprang to his feet, ripped off his sling, and charged
across the floor. He rammed his way through the Council soldiers separating House Harlan's men from House
Halarek's and grabbed Richard by the throat. He squeezed.
Hands tore at him, pulled, tugged, pried. Karne squeezed
tighter and tighter, shaking Richard at the same time, watching the head, with bulging eyes and gaping mouth, flop back
and forth. Men of his Family, with the help of Council
soldiers, finally pried Richard out of his hands. Karne
struggled against them with fierce concentration. Never
again would he have such an opportunity to end his Family's problems with House Harlan permanently. Couldn't
his cousins see that? Why did they continue dragging him
toward the Halarek benches?

"He killed her! He killed her!" Karne cried.

It took four men to keep him on the Halarek front bench. Council members took up his cry.

"He killed her!"

"Arrest the murderer!"

"Aye, arrest Harlan!"

But the chairman ordered Karne from the room and into the custody of a squad of Odonnel soldiers, who should not even have been in the Council chamber. At this blatant violation of Council protocols, even Harlan allies joined the jeers and shouts of outrage and, when the Odonnel men marched toward Karne, men of Justin and Halarek rushed to stop them. Gormsby ordered Halarek and Justin to cease resisting. He called in more soldiers. Men of many Houses reached for the knives and other weapons they had left outside the building.

The loud clash of weapons brought instant silence. Hareem Gashen stood at the back of the chamber with three squads of Council soldiers, all of them striking their ceremonial pikes and swords together. To a room full of unarmed men, even those ancient weapons were dangerous, and the fighting immediately ceased. Gashen marched the men down the aisle. One squad surrounded the Odonnel men. One squad took Richard from his Family's hands. The third followed Gashen to the chairman's table. Gashen ripped the gavel from the chairman's hand and dumped him from his chair. Gashen rapped the gavel on the desk once, sharply.

"You of the Nine Families will never again control this Council. Some of you have seen murder done and would still protect the murderer. Some of you have twisted procedure to allow a criminal—whose House has broken many laws because of its power in Council—to control vast political and financial power. The young Lharr-designate spoke truth today and at the Frosttime Council, yet you, none of you, helped him protect our world from the wolves that would destroy us."

Gashen threw long sheets of ballots on the floor in front of him. "While you mocked the law for your own clan's ends and fought on the floor of the Council chamber, we of the Freemen and minor Houses have voted and have revoked the right of the Nine to the chairmanship." He pointed to the mound of paper. "These are unanimous ballots on the Harlan trusteeship. We of the freecities and minor Houses are two-thirds of Council, my fine lords, and we vote with the young Lharr. The trusteeship continues." Gashen looked around the chamber. "The Freemen now take permanent chairmanship of this, the World Council. Look you well, and see what you have caused."

There was a rustling among the Freemen. A tall, spare man wearing the necklace of an alderman stood. "Davin Reed, freecity of Loch. Richard Harlan committed murder. We all saw."

Gashen turned to Richard. "Richard, son of House Harlan, the sentence in the law for murder is eight years in Zinn. Because you are duke-designate, you will instead serve nine years in solitary confinement at the Retreat House at Breven. Control of the affairs of your House will be in the hands of your loyal vassals until the time of your release. This sentence, too, will pass by at least two-thirds." Gashen looked at the prep tables of the Nine. "Will you test it, *Noble* Nine?"

The Nine would not. Gashen ordered Harlan arrested and taken to Breven. Richard was hauled out, punching and kicking and shouting about rights and revenge. Karne turned away from a display so embarrassingly outside Family codes of behavior.

"Let me go," he told the men who still held him. "I won't do anything else foolish."

They released him. Karne stood and faced the new chairman. "Frem Gashen, I—" Karne choked on a lump in his throat, a lump that threatened to expose his grief for all to see. "I ask to be named head-of-House now, because without regent"—he stumbled over the word, then went on—"without regent or lord much evil could happen to House Halarek between this Council and the one at midsummer. A House needs a lord, Freemen."

Gashen nodded. "Well said, young sir." He looked

around. "What is the Council's pleasure?"

Tashek, freecity of York, moved that Council approve Karne Halarek's request. The motion was adopted overwhelmingly. Relief swept through Karne, then bone-deep weariness. He felt blood seeping from the reopened slash in his arm. He knelt beside his mother, shut her eyes, and crossed her arms over her breast as custom required.

"I will rule, Lady Mother," he promised. "I'll bring our House to its proper place and power. We have help in Council now and, by your sacrifice, we have time."

He motioned two cousins to carry the Larga's body out of the chamber.

Several hours later, Karne, his sister Kathryn, and Karne's second-in-command, Nik von Schuss, returned to Ontar manor. They walked in silence through corridors hewn from bedrock and up two flights of stairs to the manor's library. In silence they stripped off their outer clothes. Kathryn sank onto the bench beside the long library table with a little sob.

"She's gone. I can't believe she's really gone. I need her so!" She crossed her arms on the table, laid her head on them, and began to cry.

Karne set his hands on her shoulders and began rubbing very lightly. "I thought she was safe," he said very softly. "At least from murder. No one's killed a woman in feud since the Sickness." His head sank forward to rest against his sister's. "Guardians! This on top of everything else!"

Karne straightened and walked to the massive stone fireplace. One wave of his hand across the fireplace logs and a convincing fire sprang up, accompanied by the scent of burning wood. Karne stared into the fire for a long time. "She died for me," he whispered finally, overwhelmed by grief and despair and ashamed of the need to let his grief out, even in front of these two, whom he trusted. "She knew the politics of this place. She knew the alliances. How can I defeat Harlan without her? Damn my sire! If I weren't so ignorant, she wouldn't have had to put herself in danger like that!"

The normally cocky Nik watched his friend for a moment, then reached over and set a hand on his shoulder. After a moment, his fingers tightened. "She gave her life to save Halarek. You are the Heir. Until you have children, you *are* Halarek. Without you, Harlan and its allies will destroy your entire Family."

"They may anyway," Karne muttered bitterly. "They've already killed most of my personal family."

Kathryn came around the table and put her arms around Karne's waist. "You've done much better than anyone expected so far."

" 'Better than anyone expected.' " Karne's bitterness deepened. "That's not saying much. People expected nothing of the 'woman' of my sire's sons. And what is 'better'? My vassals refused homage. Farm 3's serfs revolted. Harlan attacked Ontar itself—"

"For which Harlan now begins to pay," Nik reminded him.

Karne twisted out of Kit's arms. "He's not paying for that, Nik. He got off easy! And you know as well as I do that if he'd won here, no one would've mentioned that he set siege earlier than the law allows. Even the death of my lady mother would've been accepted as part of the feud if he'd done it outside Council."

"No!" Kathryn looked up at Karne with horrified eyes.

Karne stared blindly across the room at the curving iron stair that led to the upper shelves of the bookcases and to a door on the next level. He looked as if he were restraining himself from breaking something. His voice came out harsh and shaking. "Richard was sentenced to Breven because he committed murder *in the Council chamber,* Kit."

Kit shook her head. "Don't be so cynical."

"Do I have any reason not to be?"

"You'll be a better Lharr than our sire ever was!" Her tone was fierce and protective.

"Not in the eyes of this world."

Kit gripped Karne's upper arms until her knuckles whitened, ignoring his wince of pain. She gave him a hard shake. "*This* world! *This* world is backward beyond belief!

You *know* that. Mother taught us that. The Academy taught you that. What do you care what the Nine think?"

"I survive, this House survives, on what they think."

"And if they drive the Gild away? What then?"

"Starker IV does without metals or heavy equipment, among other things. Or exports, on which this House, for one, depends." Karne straightened, squared his shoulders, and took a deep breath. He pushed aside one last time the custom of keeping emotions to one's self. "I can't tell you two how much your support means to me."

The fire crackled and its scent drifted into the room. There was a long silence.

Karne swallowed hard, then made his voice brisk and firm. "We have two very important matters to take care of immediately. Kit, call in Tane and Frem Weisman. I must plan a suitable vengeance on Harlan and I must search for Egil. If Harlan's lying about not having him . . . "

Kit hurried to the com unit in the far wall.

Karne stared down at the fire. "Nik," he said, without looking up, "would you run the search for Egil? I want to look myself—Guardians, do I want to!—but I can't. House Harlan needs to be hit hard and right away if I'm to save whatever face we have left. I have to make Harlan pay, publicly, for Mother's murder or I may as well slit my throat and Kit's and let Harlan and Odonnel have this place."

There was another long silence. Everyone knew how true Karne's words were. House Halarek must punish House Harlan swiftly and severely or lose what little political power and influence it still had.

Tane Orkonan, manor secretary/manager, and his assistant, Kurt Weisman, entered. Karne put on the mask of a Gharr lord, inside and out. However, contrary to custom, Karne did not send Kit out before the men began planning how to take Harlan's outlying holdings. Karne knew well Kit could soon be the sole survivor of their personal family, and, though female, she should know how matters stood.

The search for Egil continued four months, until the storms of Uhl made further searching impossible.

CHAPTER 1

Water dripped in slow, crystalline drops from the eaves of Guardpost 105. Snow lay deep, dragging down the branches of the bluepines that surrounded the guardpost's clearing. Near the top of one of the pines, a scrawny black scavenger bird dipped and swayed on a branch that was not strong enough to hold it.

In the gun turret of the guardpost, Egil Olafsson swung the beamer in a horizontal arc, using his forearms. He squinted against the glare from the snow. At the moment, none of the quick, emaciated shadows that were the Runners showed themselves, but they were still out there. He knew they were still out there. He risked a quick check on Karne's progress by lifting his nose from the beamer's activator button and looking toward the pass. A tiny figure stood at its very rim, looking back. Egil felt a surge of pride; without hands, he had still made it possible for Karne to reach the boundary of Zinn. The figure at the rim of the pass raised one arm in a salute of thanks and farewell, then turned, exposing the wide blue collar Halarek men had always worn in battle, and disappeared over the top of the pass.

Blood brother and friend. They would see each other no more. "Goodbye," Egil murmured. "May Thor and Odin aid you, though I know you don't believe in them.

Tell your children how your friend Egil saved your life by holding off hordes of Runners single-handedly." Egil looked down at his hands, frozen into numb, useless lumps. "Single-nosedly," he amended.

"Hordes" was also, perhaps, inaccurate. He admitted that. But his stand, alone, against the worst criminals of Starker IV, was worthy of a lay, maybe even part of a saga. Those allowed some embroidery of facts. Beowulf. Sigurd Dragon-slayer. Artos. Those had had to be embroidered. Heimdal defending Bifrost. Egil Olafsson at the Desert of Zinn, holding the Runners at bay so his brother-by-choice could live to tell Council about Harlan's new treachery. The struggle of Karne Halarek to defend his territory against far stronger enemies—that was saga material if anything was and appearing in a saga would put Egil finally on the same level as Solveig and Einar and Hring and Hadd.

Egil shook his head. Perhaps he had been reaching too high, but what else could he do? He had not the amazing academic abilities of Donner and Kenner, and his Academy grades had showed it. There was no possibility at all he could open a centuries-closed world to trade like Hadd did, nor invent starship parts like Hring. He could not even advance rapidly in the navy like Einar. And Solveig—Solveig was a sybil and that was fame enough for two or three people. He was the only one of the Olafsson children who had not already earned either fame or fortune. Even the three younger than he had. Egil wondered if Horatio or Beowulf or Siegfried had dreamed of fame as he did, or felt the doubts and fear and frustration. He wondered if Karne did. Karne's sire had publicly showed his contempt for his third son. He had not loved Karne, perhaps had not liked him at all. Trev Halarek thought only big, brawny men like himself were really *men*. Only those who relished fighting and intrigues and war were really *men*. Karne, born third of Trev's four sons, had had the ill luck to be slender and wiry like his mother. To compound the problem, Karne had early shown that he valued learning, diplomacy, and negotiation, as the Larga did. For these reasons, Trev had despised his third son and had even passed over him in the line of inheritance to make his fourth son, Liam, the third in line. Only her femaleness kept Trev from putting Kit ahead, too. Her wiry slenderness and love of learning were all right because she was female.

Odin Olafsson was not like that at all. He loved all his children well and had grown to love Karne, too. But Egil always felt like the runt of the litter, and all his father's assurances that he was "just a late bloomer" did not help.

Out of the corner of his eye, Egil saw a shadow creeping toward the guardpost. He swung the beamer and pressed the activator with his nose. A brilliant stream of light shot across the clearing, and the shadow scurried back into the shelter of the trees. Across the clearing, at the beam's end, a bluepine's branches sprang upward as the snow on them vaporized. A fraction of a second later, the tree itself exploded.

Egil gave a grunt of disgust. Missed him. *If my hands were working—*

The anger was on him, sudden and powerful. He had had a chance to acquire honor and fame by taking vengeance for Harlan treacheries against Karne. Now, thanks to another treachery, an illegal siege, Egil had no hands with which to keep his oath of vengeance. Hunted through the freezing night by Harlan fliers, crouching over tiny fires trying to warm hands that would not warm, knowing the hands were dead, closing off even the small fame of life as a harper or painter—"May Fenris Wolf eat your heart, Richard Harlan!" Egil snarled.

A Runner dashed toward the guard hut. Egil spun, aimed, and fired. The skinny man collapsed in the snow.

They'll get in in time, Egil told himself. Gissen won't fight. He may even let them in.

Egil spared only that moment's thought for the whining soldier whom Karne had left behind to feed him and help him with the necessities of life.

A cluster of Runners dashed across the clearing and Egil sprayed them with the beamer. Three fell.

At least death would earn fame. A lay, a small saga . . .

Then Egil remembered. The Gharr thought music frivolous and effeminate and poetry a waste of time. The Gharr also relied too often on political maneuvering, ambushes, and assassins to be considered honorable in war, so they had no respect for honor, and they had no arts or diplomacy to speak of, either. No, there would be no saga or lay made from this adventure, not on this world. At home, maybe, if sybils could See worlds away—

A tall thin shape crept toward the hut, using shadows under the trees as cover. Egil sent a beamer bolt after it. The shape staggered but did not fall. Out of the corner of his eye, Egil caught movement on the other side of the clearing. He spun the beamer. A crowd of gaunt figures rushed from the protecting shadows and swarmed toward the guardpost. Egil fired rapidly. More came from another direction. Egil spun the firing chair one way and then another. A Runner fell here, another there, another over there, but there were too many of them, and too many had gotten so close to the guardpost they were no longer in range. Something slammed into the door below. It sounded like some kind of battering ram. Egil pushed himself out of the chair and shook his shoulders to loosen them. He heard a terrified yelp and then a clatter at the foot of the stairs. Egil wondered briefly what Gissen was doing. Running to him for protection? He looked down again at his frozen hands. They would protect no one.

The door below gave with a splintering crash. There was a clamor of voices, a short, high-pitched screech of terror. Then the infamous, eerie howl of the Runners began below, a chilling cry of triumph.

"That's it for Gissen," Egil muttered.

Egil glanced quickly around the room. There was nothing he could use as a weapon. The lift's motor began to hum. Egil laughed harshly. Even if there had been a weapon, he could not have held it, and, without hands, his Drinn wrestling skills were useless, too. The lift's motor stopped. Egil squared his shoulders. He would use the hands themselves as weapons. If that use damaged them more, it would not matter, for he would not live out the hour, but he would die as a warrior should, fighting. At least the gods had granted him that much. He turned to face the lift door.

It opened and a pack of gaunt men burst into the tiny gun turret. Egil met them swinging his leaden hands. The men fell back for a moment, perhaps in amazement. Egil smashed a fist into a face and heard teeth crunch. The men surged forward. Egil kicked at them to make them keep their distance. Two Runners grabbed for his arms. Egil twisted and ducked. Another cluster of Runners got out of the lift.

Too many. Too many.

He swung his arms like clubs and twisted and kicked and spun, but even with the strength that years of Drinn had given him, they were too many. The Runners swarmed over him and bore him to the floor. Egil gasped for breath under the weight of them. There were so many bodies, they shut out the light. Egil heaved and struggled. He felt a savage pain on the side of his head, then everything went dark and silent.

Zigzags of searing light pierced the darkness. Egil came aware slowly. There was cold and hardness and an awful silence. Had he gone to Hel even though he had fallen in battle? He opened his eyes reluctantly. It was dusk, and he was lying facedown on red-brown tiles. He hit the tiles with one wooden hand.

"I'm still alive! Those skinny sons of Loki have denied me my one chance to die a warrior!"

He listened. Nothing, no one responded to his angry shout. He was alone, then, and he knew next to nothing about the geography of Starker IV. Then Egil noticed the dusk was not just quiet, there was no sound at all—not of dripping water from the thaw, not of falling snow, not of the Runners themselves. Cautiously, painfully, Egil rolled over and sat up. The tiles belonged to a vast circular pavement, cracked in places, broken away in others, and snowless. Just beyond the tiles, snow drifted knee-deep. To his right, in the center of the pavement, was a large pile of ashes and a larger pile of wind-fallen wood and cut branches. Beyond the ashes, painted on the tile, was the leaf symbol the people of Starker IV used to represent the Watchers.

Egil felt a cold rush of fear. This was a Place of Leaving. A place where the Runners left sacrifices for their gods, the Watchers. Karne had told him about such places. The Watchers lit fires to guide the Runners to their prey. Egil himself had seen those fires in the mountains after the Harlan soldiers had driven them to the edge of Zinn. Egil looked at the ashes again. Perhaps this was not one of the Watchers' fires. Perhaps fires in a Place of Leaving had another purpose altogether. Perhaps they called the Watchers to the sacrifice. Perhaps they burned the sacrifice.

He scrambled to his feet as best he could with dead and useless hands. Out. He would get out before the Watchers, whatever they were, came. But his feet were numb from cold. He stumbled more than walked toward the edge of the pavement and the snow beyond it. The detail finally registered. There was snow beyond the pavement but not on it. There had to be some sort of wall, then, an invisible wall. Egil reached the edge and put out his arms ahead of him. Though his hands could not feel the barrier, his arms felt resistance. He reached higher, then lower. The resistance was the same. He walked along the edge of the pavement in one direction and then in the other. Everywhere the invisible resistance. He pushed hard. The barrier did not give. He pushed with all his strength, and still nothing happened. He looked over his shoulder at the pile of ashes and at the wood ready for another fire. He shook his head. He would not wait to be a sacrifice.

Egil slammed his shoulder into the wall with all his strength. A blinding, shuddering shock ran through him, then all went black.

Warmth, and a low murmur of voices, told Egil he was in yet another place. He opened his eyelids just a slit, so whoever was near him would not know he was awake. He saw nothing but a brightness overhead. He feigned a waking-up groan and rolled onto his side, or, more exactly, he attempted to roll onto his side. Something fastened his arms to the surface he was lying on. His eyes flew open, and he heaved upward against the bonds with a roar of anger and frustration.

Before his voice stopped echoing, two sets of hands had pressed him firmly back onto the flat surface on which he was lying. Egil twisted his head back and around to see who was with him. He saw a gray rock wall and folds of blue fabric belted with leather and—

Egil suddenly realized his fingers were aiding his movement by gripping the mattress or covering he lay on. He stopped struggling. He rubbed his fingertips against the cloth beneath them. He could *feel* the coarse texture! Hands released the restraints. He lay still a moment, then slowly lifted his hands, and looked at them. He wiggled his fingers. He stroked one hand with the other. They moved! They felt!

"My hands," he whispered.

"Aye, but you must be careful of them for a while yet. They are not—finished." The voice belonged to a woman and spoke the saga-language of Balder.

Egil looked up. The woman stood at one side of his bed, a man near the head. The woman was tall and elegant, and her hair was paling from blond to silver-gray. The man was as tall, with a head of red hair and a bristling beard to match. They both had the pale skin and blue eyes of Balder. To be home, after months of living with the small, brown Gharr under the surface of their bitter-cold world, was too much for Egil to bear without shouting his joy.

The inarticulate cry roared back at him, bouncing again and again from the stone walls, indicating what must be a very large room. He looked around. The gray walls curved upward and overhead to form a cave-like ceiling. The room itself was huge, like a cave, and had several doorways that opened into what looked like tunnels.

Sudden doubt wiped out Egil's joy. This couldn't be Balder. The people looked the same, but no one lived underground like this on Balder. There was no reason to. If this were Balder, there would be windows, big windows, and bright, clear sunlit air outside them. And his hands worked. Another reason this could not be Balder. His hands had been frozen. Dead. Now they were alive and working again. No doctors on Balder had that much skill. But the people were of the Viking kind, like him, and that meant . . . Egil shook his head as if that could shake this puzzle into understandable shapes. His confusion must have shown on his face.

The woman said gently, "This is a surprise, no? To find the Viking kind here? The Gharr couldn't tell you. The Gharr don't know."

The redheaded man chuckled. "The Gharr live in such willful ignorance. There is more besides us to this world that the mighty Gharr lords know nothing about. But I can understand your confusion."

"We're on Starker IV?" Egil blurted.

The man laughed again. "Of course. Does this look like Balder?" He waved his arm toward the cave room. "And I'm forgetting my courtesies. You have been with us so long, Egil, that I forget you don't know who we are. Our forebears were Balder colonists who landed astray. I am Magnus the Red, son of Thorbjorn, son of Gaill."

"And I am Frigdis, daughter of Finboggis, son of Halli."

"Not on Balder," Egil repeated, still feeling confused and rather stupid. "You're of the Viking kind, too, and yet we're not on Balder?"

Both shook their heads.

The woman's face softened in sympathy. "We told you. We *are* your people." She motioned for Egil to get up and come with her. "Come. It's mealtime. We can explain as we go." Frigdis turned and walked briskly toward a dark doorway across the huge room.

When Egil sat up, he felt the soft brush of beard against his throat and chest. He reached up tentatively and touched his face. The beard he had been so proud of, the beard he had removed to live with the clean-shaven Gharr, had grown back and was two fingers long. He had been asleep a long time! Egil stepped down from the bed's platform and followed Frigdis. Magnus fell into step beside him. Egil's hosts paused in the doorway. The tunnel beyond brightened slowly.

"Look now," Frigdis said. "Our community is laid out

very efficiently, considering it started in caves, but you still must recognize rooms and tunnels to find your way around."

Egil looked at the big room. Narrow channels in the walls and floor led trickles of water to a smooth black pool at the room's center. Benches stood at the edge of the pool, curved to match its contours, and small trees stood in tubs at each bench's ends. Some sort of glowing fixtures kept the room bright as day. He looked across the room at the bed-platform where he had lain. Other such platforms lined the wall on that side of the roughly circular room and two or three of them were occupied. This was, or had been, a natural cave, slightly altered to even contours. Here and there on the walls places had been smoothed flat and decorated with paintings, mosaics, or raised sculptures depicting stories from the sagas or the lives of the gods. The floor, cut to look as if it were set with stone tiles, had been polished as smooth and shining as glass. The effect of tiles was so real that the artist in Egil knelt and felt the crack between two "tiles" where a small piece of grout had fallen out; the "tile" was truly part of the bedrock. His fingers could *feel* the difference. His fingers could feel!

Egil stood slowly. He was alive. He was with his own people and still on Starker IV. Most amazing of all, he had his hands back! His fingers were warm again. They moved. They felt. Egil touched his fingertips to each other, then shook off the feeling of stunned amazement. There would be plenty of time to think about what had happened, plenty of time to talk when he was back at Ontar. Karne and Kit and Nik would be so glad to see him!

Frigdis touched his arm lightly. "Have you looked enough?" When Egil nodded, Frigdis stepped into the tunnel and walked briskly away.

Magnus cleared his throat.

He wants to start our conversation up again, Egil thought. Knowing how to read that sort of behavior is one of the few useful things I learned at the Academy. Karne did much better. He would've—

"Surely there must be legends of lost ships on Balder, Egil."

Egil nodded politely. There were several. Every colonial world had lost ships. And worlds such as Balder, founded by splinter groups wanting to launch a special way of life, perhaps had more lost-ship tales than the average. But that was not what he wanted to talk about right then.

Magnus continued, oblivious to Egil's polite disinterest. "Our ancestors' ship crashed here about two thousand years ago. The longflight was new then, and chancy, and there was no way to find, let alone rescue, ships that got lost or crashed. So, perforce, our people stayed and—"

Egil touched Magnus's sleeve respectfully but firmly. "Gentlehom, how did I come here? Last I remember I was in a Place of Leaving."

The redheaded man nodded. "Most of our guests arrive as you did. There is—a method of transportation centered on those places. And the Runners sometimes use them to leave us gifts, in return for our signals that someone has entered the Desert. The signals help newcomers survive. A little. A very few other guests somehow survive passage through one of our tunnels to the Upper World."

Egil stopped dead still. These were the Watchers! These descendants of strayed Balder colonists were the Watchers, the beings the Gharr thought were the gods of the Runners! The Watchers were Egil's own people!

There was so much astonishing new information that Egil needed several minutes of quiet to absorb what he had just learned and he knew he was not going to get those minutes. Finally he had to confirm his guess. "You're the Watchers."

Magnus gave a short nod.

Egil gripped Magnus's arm to stop him from moving on down the tunnel. "I must go back. If you can have the power to bring people and things from a Place of Leaving, if you can bring me, you can send me back. Karne Halarek needs me. Send me back now!"

Magnus and Frigdis looked at each other in dismay.

Egil felt a prickle of unease.

"I must go back. I've sworn to stand by him until his war is over or until one of us is dead." He turned toward the room they had just left. "Where are the rest of my things?"

Neither Magnus nor Frigdis said anything.

"I appreciate your care for me," Egil added hastily. "There's no way I can ever repay you for the return of my hands, but Karne's my brother-by-choice. Surely you understand what that means."

Magnus glanced at Frigdis. "It sounds like a boys' romantic fantasy to me. How old are you and your friend? No, forget that. The Halarek came of age in the spring. I Saw the ceremony. You're both only eighteen."

Egil's face felt hot and he was grateful he did not blush. "Only eighteen! Karne's responsible for several thousand lives! Sigurd and Artos were—"

"The ancient heroes did their deeds at sixteen and eighteen and nineteen and twenty and were *dead* by the time they were twenty-five or thirty. Times were different. Grow up! I have no patience with romantics. Too many people get hurt." Magnus sped up, passed Frigdis, and disappeared around a bend in the tunnel.

"The Halarek and his troubles aren't the problem with sending you back, Egil," Frigdis said gently, her eyes following Magnus. "Magnus is very sensitive about such dreams because both his father and grandfather died on what Magnus considers 'foolish, romantic adventures.' Talk to the godi about your oath. The godi listens to petitions after every meal."

Egil nodded. That was reasonable. A community's godi was priest and mayor and war leader. The godi would understand oaths and honor. Yet Egil's need to get back to the fighting rode him like a demon.

"But every day Karne's situation grows worse—"

Frigdis's voice was suddenly cool and stiff. "You have been asleep since nine Verdain, Gharr time, Egil. It is now the beginning of Arhast. Your friend came of age in Aden and has been managing his own problems."

Two hundred days. Five months. He had been "asleep" five months! His healing had taken more than half a year! It was too much to absorb. Frigdis spoke to him after that, but he understood nothing but the sound of her voice.

Five months. Karne could have lost everything in five months.

Frigdis stopped Egil in the doorway of a very large room, similar to the one where Egil had awakened, by a jerk on his sleeve. Long tables filled a good part of the open space. A great number of people sat along benches on either side of these tables, eating what looked like a generous meal. Most of the diners were big and fair, but there were also many Runners, several serfs or slaves, though it was hard to tell which beyond that they were smaller than others of the Gharr, and a swarthy woman Egil would have sworn was a native of Rigel. At the center of the long table nearest the cave wall, a brawny man with graying beard and hair sat in the high seat, a chair with a tall, carved back supported by even taller carved posts, each topped with a stylized raven. Magnus was standing beside the chair. The godi looked Egil over carefully with piercing blue eyes.

"So, our new guest is awake." The man's voice was deep and his tone courteous.

"He wants to know how matters go with his brother-by-rite, the Lharr Halarek," Magnus said.

Egil wanted to say that was *not* what he had asked for, but thought better of it.

"He does, does he?" The big man examined Egil again. He nodded slowly. "All in good time, young man, all in good time. Have a seat"—the man waved toward the end of his table—"and join us at meat." And he smiled at his silly rhyme. "We treat guests well here. Go, sit, enjoy your first real meal with us."

Frigdis touched Egil's elbow. "*After* the meal."

Egil shook off her hand and looked hard at the godi. "I don't wish to be discourteous, gentlehom, but I don't have a lot of time. Karne is surrounded by powerful enemies who may any day conquer his House and take his life. I've sworn to stand with him. I must return to do that now I'm whole again. Vengeance has always been our right and our duty. Don't you understand that here?"

"We remember." The godi looked at Egil hard, then at

Magnus. "Did you tell him the healing is not yet complete?"

"Aye, I told him."

"Aught else?"

"Naught to the point."

The godi nodded thoughtfully, then he set his piercing eyes on Egil again. "I'm sorry this was not explained to you at once." He waved a hand toward the far table where the Runners and the Rigellian sat. "They are our guests. You are our guest. You may have of us whatever you wish that we can provide, but you cannot leave. Ever. The people of the Upper World, whom you call the Gharr, do not know we exist. They must never know we exist. You cannot leave."

CHAPTER 2

Egil stiffened. "You intend to keep me against my will?"

"No one leaves." The godi's eyes narrowed. "No one has ever left. No one has ever escaped. Those who come to us through the tunnels (mostly Runners and serfs, as you can see) have hidden in them out of desperation and work their way downward." He nodded toward the tables where the "guests" sat. "Only about ten percent survive the traps and hazards. It's asking too much to expect any of that small percentage to survive a return trip. No one has." He returned his attention to his meal.

Egil's first urge was to grab the godi by his beard and jerk his head up to make him pay attention. His fists clenched instead. It would not help at all to attack the chief of this place. He turned slowly away. He watched the tight lines in Frigdis's face ease. She touched his arm lightly in approval, then motioned toward some empty places near the end of the table.

They sat. Food was passed, introductions made, food consumed, but Egil was barely aware of what was happening. The godi's words had been like a boot in his gut, and Egil felt numb with shock. He touched neither his tankard nor his food.

I'm trapped here. Karne must fight alone, die alone, and I'll die here, remembered only as the "runt" of the Olafsson litter.

"Runt" stung. Though Egil knew his father and brothers meant it only as teasing, it had always stung, and that reminded Egil of the hostility the people of the Houses felt toward Karne, whom they knew only through his sire. Trev Halarek had called Karne "weak" and "womanish," both great insults in Gharr eyes. Egil shook his head. The tough, wiry boy who had come to the Academy six years before had been neither weak nor womanish, only stunned and confused by the differences between life on Starker IV and on a world of the Federation. He had quickly won respect for his nerve, persistence, honesty, and quick intelligence. And the girls, ah, the girls . . .

Egil looked down at the chunk of meat and pile of steaming vegetables on his plate. The sight turned his normally cast-iron stomach. He had come here with the dream of winning glory and fame in battle. Egil remembered the battle over his going, the only serious quarrel he and his father had ever had.

"You're giving up a naval career to fight a war that's not yours?" his father had said. "A war that's been going on for generations and will likely run generations more? Egil, one more man in Karne's army, big as you are compared to them, isn't going to make a bit of difference. Thor's Hammer! I know how much you like Karne. I like him a lot myself, but he needs an *army*, Egil!"

"He needs a *friend*, Dad. On Starker IV, no lord dares trust his 'friends.' I can give advice Karne won't need to examine with a magnifier to see what my Family's interest is or what I'll gain from it."

"But you will gain from it, or hope you will, right? You're out to win a name for yourself and you don't need to. You'll find your own gifts in time. It's not necessary to do this."

"It's necessary for me."

"Then think of this. The world Thing outlawed war for good reasons. The Inner Worlds have given up war for good reasons."

" 'Cattle die, kinsmen die, even you yourself—' "

"Don't quote at me, you self-serving young fool! What good is fame if you're dead?"

"It would be better to be dead than to be laughed at! 'Your brothers did so and so and so. What happened to you?' People have been saying things like that to me for *years*, Dad."

The battle raged for hours, but Egil had won his ticket to Starker IV in the end. To no point now. His only reason for coming to this cold and barbarous world was his oath to his friend and he would now never be able to keep it. Well, to be honest, his oath was not the only reason. To be really honest, maybe not even the most important reason.

Egil slammed his fist down beside his plate. Intense pain lanced up his arm and flooded out the rage he felt at his own helplessness. Egil shut his eyes tight and cradled the injured fist in his other hand, hoping he would not cry out with the agony of it. When the pain became bearable, Egil spun his seat away from the table and stood, his only thought to get out somehow, to find a way out and back to Halarek Holding and the keeping of his oath. He had come to Halarek Holding under false pretenses, but he would make up for that dishonesty one way or another.

He had gone only two or three steps before Magnus was beside him, gripping his arm hard enough to make him stand still. "We don't want you to die, young man. We do not lie when we say there is no escape."

"Are you telepaths, too?" Egil felt the bitterness of that on his tongue. Not even his thoughts were private.

Magnus's mouth twisted downward. "Nay. We don't need to read minds to know what you're thinking. Many guests before you have thought we were lying, or that there had to be some flaw in our protection, or that they were smart enough to outwit the traps."

Magnus released Egil's arm and glanced toward the godi. The godi nodded once and returned to his beer and the conversation with his neighbor.

"Come." The word was an order, not an invitation. "We'll take care of your doubts right now." Magnus walked briskly toward a tunnel mouth. "Two days ago a Runner guest decided he had to go back to the Desert."

Egil hesitated only a moment. Perhaps he really could not bull his way out. Perhaps he needed time to study the

Watchers and their tunnels. For a while he would do as they said, starting now. He would watch, listen, and find a way out. There had to be a way out. After all, the Watchers helped the Runners in the Upper World. They themselves had said so. So there had to be a way out.

Magnus led through tunnel after intersecting tunnel, each brightening as they approached and dimming after they passed. Though Egil had tried at the beginning to keep track of the turns and twists and intersections, he eventually gave up. He would have to make a map or mark safe areas in another way. He did continue doggedly counting his steps, though.

Suddenly Magnus halted. "From here, you must follow my example exactly," he said. "Exactly." He studied Egil's face a long moment. "I know how hard the Viking kind find following someone else's orders. The sagas are full of examples. But if you don't do exactly as I do, you won't live to eat your dessert."

That was clear enough. Egil looked at the tunnel ahead of them. It looked like the stretch of tunnel they had just come through. He looked at Magnus. There was no reason for the man to lie to him. He hadn't walked all this way to play a joke on the new "guest." Egil nodded.

"Stay right behind me," Magnus ordered. He walked forward about two meters, stepped abruptly two long steps to his left, walked forward two steps, stepped right one long step, and stopped.

When Egil was beside him, Magnus lay on the stone floor, held on to an iron ring at the base of the wall, then pounded with his free fist on the space he had just stepped around. The floor fell away with a hollow bang, and something, perhaps a small piece of loose masonry, clittered across that piece of floor, then, after a long silence, fell into water far below. The *plop* it made as it hit was very faint.

"Perhaps the Runner used a different tunnel. Perhaps he was very thin and ran very fast. Sometimes a light, fast runner, sticking right against the walls, can pass this sort of trap. So we have others." Magnus stood and moved on.

Two hundred paces farther, Magnus stopped and ran his hand up and down the stone wall. "Feel here. There are two tiny cracks about an arm's length apart. Find them?"

Egil nodded.

"I won't demonstrate this, because it takes too long to put back. There is a matching set of cracks about two meters farther on. These are sections of wall that slide out in a fraction of a second, trapping an escapee between them. The small area in between quickly runs out of breathable air . . . " He looked at Egil.

"I get the idea," Egil said dryly.

Magnus's mouth twitched. He took a small round device from a pocket, pressed a button on it, and held the button down while the two men crossed through the trap. Magnus indicated the trap behind them with a jerk of his head. "That we didn't find the Runner here supports my guess that he came to his death place by different passages. I'll show you one more of the traps, and then I'll show you the Runner. Or what's left of him."

Five hundred thirty paces farther Magnus stopped again, tipped a heavy wooden plank across a section of floor, and crossed to the other side. "Sometimes we want to go out," he explained, motioning to the plank.

After Egil joined him, Magnus turned, picked up the plank, and rapped its end hard against the section of floor he had just crossed. The floor fell away silently. Magnus shined a pocket light into the hole. The hole was about three meters deep. Metal stakes, positioned only a hand's breadth apart, covered the floor of the trap.

"This trap opens by vibrations on this side. That's why it's silent. The intruder takes one more step and—" His hand dropped vigorously downward.

"But if—"

"If the intruder has a light, the light will not help, because the trap feels vibrations only a step or two from the edge. By that time, the light is shining farther down the tunnel. Even if it were pointed down, just ahead of the intruder's feet, it would be too late; he would have to stop so quickly he would overbalance and fall in, anyway."

Egil shuddered. To think the floor was solid and safe and then to fall in there . . . At least it would be a quicker death than dropping into the deep well. He jerked his thoughts back into line and followed Magnus, paying very careful attention to exactly what the man did.

Eight hundred twenty-seven paces and two right turns (one sharp, one shallow) later, a huge block of masonry closed off the tunnel. Even without the aid of the hand light, Egil could see the sprawled and bloody legs protruding from the underside of the stone. One of them had been ripped away below the knee.

Egil looked away, up at the top of the massive stone booby. Magnus noticed.

"Zinn bear," he said. "Sometimes they come in if they smell fresh meat. They seem to sense the floor traps and leap over them, so it's only boobies like this that will get a bear. We don't want them coming in, either." He shined the light at the roof of the tunnel. "The stone must be lifted back into place by a complicated arrangement of winches and pulleys. That's why it's still in the tunnel and not in the ceiling where it belongs. This is one of the outer traps in this tunnel."

Egil could not understand how Magnus could talk so calmly about devices that killed people horribly.

Magnus looked at the sprawled legs. "I can't understand why anyone would prefer a Runner's life to living here, especially since he had only completed four months of his seven-year sentence." He turned to Egil. "Did you know only a few convicts survive their first winter in Zinn?"

Egil shook his head.

"That's why the sentences are so short. Those that survive even one year in the Desert are never the same. The Gharr allow them back into ordinary life afterward with no worry that they will ever commit another crime." Magnus touched the Runner's shabby remaining boot with his toe. "This poor soul had a long time to go. Seven years is the longest sentence they hand out, except for murder." He looked up. "Perhaps he considered this a better choice than either of the others. Perhaps he never intended to get to the Upper World."

Magnus studied Egil. "Suppose you *could* get to the surface, which you cannot. It's Arhast up there. Even if it were midsummer, you don't know the country, you don't know the local stars, you have no supplies, and you're from a warm-weather world. Even midsummer here is much cooler than you are accustomed to."

Egil remembered the bitter cold of Zinn in Verdain. Could he find Halarek Holding without familiar constellations to guide him? If he could, how long would it take? Weeks? Months? During Arhast, Koort, and Nemb, the Gharr did not go outside at all, because nothing survived the searing cold and vicious winds. But the Runner had tried. Egil understood why the man chose death instead of endless imprisonment, though Magnus did not seem to. The centuries underground had taken from the Watchers the Viking love of fresh air and open space and few rules. A true Viking would die rather than live unfree. He himself had chosen to die fighting rather than live with useless hands or submit mildly to whatever the Runners could do to him.

Egil looked down at his hands, closed the fingers, opened them, closed them, opened them. He had his hands back. He could paint again, pilot again. He could fight. He could teach Karne's men Drinn holds now, holds that killed faster than weapons. He could take Richard Harlan's hands in return for the destruction of his. That was the law. Weregeld, the permissible compensation for injury, he would not accept, even if the Gharr understood what weregeld was, which they did not. But he could do none of those things imprisoned down here.

"Are you coming, or would you rather come alone later and become a people-pattie like that Runner?" Magnus's voice cut through Egil's thoughts like a saw. "I want to finish my dinner."

Egil wondered just how long he had been staring at the rock. Magnus had seriously shaken his confidence in his ability to escape. Magnus was now a little way along the tunnel looking back at him, every line of his body showing impatience. Egil followed, keeping his mind tightly on the following in order to stay alive.

The tunnel looked different than it had coming out. It was different: They returned to the Great Hall through a different door and in much less time than it had taken to make the outbound trip. That meant they had taken a different path and *that* nullified all Egil's careful counting. Egil was quite sure, from the sly look Magnus gave him, that the change had been made to do precisely that.

Magnus led Egil back to the godi's highseat. "He has seen, lord, what there is to see."

The godi nodded dismissal to Magnus, then turned to Egil. "You have seen. No one has escaped this place in all the two thousand years the traps have been here. No one will stop you from trying to leave, but we strongly advise against it." The godi nodded dismissal and returned his attention to his dessert.

The woman who sat beside the godi handed Egil a piece of paper. "The directions to your assigned quarters, Egil Odin's son," was all she said before she turned her attention to the woman sitting to her left.

Egil looked at the paper. It was a rudimentary map. He looked at the meat and vegetables on his plate, now cold. He felt no more like eating them than before. But a bowl of pudding now sat above his plate. The pudding was thick and a warm, glistening brown. A pudding such as his mother made. He sat down and spooned up a bite. The smooth mound in the spoon felt unusually heavy. It was also unusually good. Egil rapidly finished the pudding and reached for a tankard of beer to wash it down.

His hand would not grip the tankard firmly, and the tankard crashed onto the table, scattering pottery fragments and beer on Egil and his neighbors. Egil sat, stunned, while one of the table servers mopped up the mess. Though Egil remembered Frigdis warning him that his hands were not yet "finished," he had not understood what she meant. Fear raced through him, making him feel weak and sick. If it had taken almost five months to heal them this much, how much longer until they were back to full strength? Would they ever regain full strength?

A new wave of fear made Egil so wobbly that he had

to brace his hands against the table to keep from falling over. He had had such hopes when he felt the bedcover, moved his fingers, gripped with hands he had lost. Would he be able to hold a brush long enough to finish a painting? Could he ever again do things as simple as lifting a child, or throwing a man with a Drinn hold, or picking up his own beer? He was astonished that he could have built the return of hands into so much in so short a time. But he had, and the thought of perhaps never being normal again was almost too much to bear.

In spite of both the godi's words and the convincing tunnel tour, Egil was determined to find a way out. There had to be a safe way out if the Watchers went Above at all, and they did. As if to prove his belief, the Watchers kept a close eye on Egil, an ostentatiously close eye. When he spent several days exploring the living areas of the colony, no one stopped him, but someone followed him at a discreet distance. Someone else always followed him to the cubicle assigned him. During the nights, others watched outside his door. For a time, Egil thought this was funny, but then he saw their motive: They remembered that it was better to die than to break oath with a friend. They remembered it was better to die than let an injury go unavenged.

He was not yet ready to die, however. Clearly there would be no easy bolting from this place, but there *had* to be a way out.

Egil quickly settled himself into a routine. He hoped such a routine would convince the Watchers he had resigned himself to staying. Egil arranged physical workouts, reading, and, as his hands grew stronger, painting, around the two meals and the seven-hour period of darkness in each Watcher "day." The Watchers willingly supplied Egil with all the art supplies he could want and access to their library and several pools for swimming.

Two of the long Gharr weeks passed. Because his painting was not going well, Egil spent lots of time reading. Soon he had read most of the colony's history and a good deal about the flora and fauna of Starker IV. He could paint the "horses," the bluepines and fire trees, the mountain wildflowers and the long-haired squirrels, but what he wanted to paint was a portrait, and without its model the painting refused to develop into a likeness of her.

Egil had been tinkering with the portrait for days. The girl in it looked out with warm golden eyes. Her dark hair, tied back with a blue ribbon, resisted even that much discipline in a tangle of waves and soft curls. A long tendril rested in a half-curl against her brown cheek.

"She's a pretty girl, she's a likable girl," Egil muttered. "Days I've worked on this, and she still isn't Kit! She hasn't got Kit's spark!" He raised his arm to throw the brush down in disgust, then thought of the splotch the paint would make and the bother of cleaning up the mess. He lowered his arm and began cleaning the brush. Kit Halarek was out of his reach in more ways than one.

The mess cleaned up and supplies put away, Egil went tunnel-exploring. The tunnels near the living quarters held no traps and were marked with stripes of paint that were codes for their destinations. The tunnels to the Upper World were marked with fluorescent X's and signs that told their destinations. Egil learned from these that there were tunnels under the Holdings of all the Nine Houses and many of the minor Holdings. Most of these had exits in the ruins of surface buildings or villages, early attempts by Watchers or Gharr to live on the surface. In addition, the Retreat Houses, also remnants of Watchers' surface life, each had hidden passages at their lowest levels that connected to the Watchers tunnels. These had originally been built for safety from severe weather, or so Magnus had told him.

In the following days, Egil carefully drew maps of the Watchers' living areas and tunnels. The Rigellian woman often watched him pacing off distances and drawing. He learned her name was Aneala Yrrondnikk. She was a Gildswoman who had become a "guest" through her hobby, archeology. She had been exploring deep under a ruin left by the Old Ones when one of the boobies with spikes had opened in front of her. With the well-known agility of her race, she had twisted around quickly enough to grab the edge of the pit and hang on. Many hours later, maintenance workers, coming to reset the trap, had rescued her.

The woman watched him drawing his maps for more than a week before she approached him in the great hall one evening. Egil had raised a full tankard of beer without dropping it, and then two. He was feeling very good about himself and his hands and beer. Aneala came up silently behind him and spoke by his ear.

"I want to get out. You want to get out. I have knowledge. You have knowledge. Will you come aside to talk with me about this?"

Egil needed only a moment to consider. She might have information he could use. If not, what was a few minutes out of a lifetime down here? He rose from the table and followed her into an empty tunnel.

She began speaking as soon as they were out of earshot of the diners. "Those others"—she waved a hand disdainfully toward the other guests—"believe what they've been told. Besides, for most of them is this a far better life, although see they never the sun, than could they expect wherever they came from. Me, I have work to get back to. At least, I hope I have work to get back to. People and places to see. I have been down here a year, as best I can guess— they have ten-day weeks here, no?—and was I in line to be promoted off this backwater world this past spring."

Egil looked down at her curiously. If she was in such a hurry, why had she not acted sooner? "What do you want of me?"

"You've made maps. You can read the language here. I know the floor traps. I've studied them for a year. We can help each other."

Egil pursed his mouth thoughtfully. He had no doubt it was the translation she was after. What was the harm? They weren't competitors. He nodded. "I don't have the maps with me, of course. I'll meet you in the library after daymeal tomorrow. All right?"

She nodded.

Egil had the maps spread on a clean table by the time Aneala came the next day. He ran a hand over them to smooth them and pointed to the library on one map. Tunnel entrances on two sides were marked, but nothing else about those tunnels was shown.

Egil pointed to the blank space. "As you can see, I'm nowhere near ready to leave. Among my people, it is better to die fighting or trying to escape than to live in prison, without taking vengeance, or of old age. The real problem for me with dying is I swore an oath to my brother-by-choice—do you understand brother-by-choice?"

The woman nodded. "A rite. An exchange of blood."

Egil continued. "I swore to protect him until death, his or mine. As long as I live, I must carry out that oath or be dishonored in the eyes of my family and all who know me. My family is much accomplished and very well known. The disgrace of being related to an oath-breaker would be great. I can't fulfill my oaths down here. That's clear. I'm sure my friend thinks I'm dead, so in his eyes I've lost no honor, but my mother and sister are sybils. There are other sybils on Balder, so what I do here is not secret there. *They* know I'm not defending my friend. *I* know it. I must try to do as I swore I would or die trying."

Egil stared down at the maps for a long moment and with a finger traced one long tunnel as far as a giant red X. "I now believe what the godi and Magnus say. There really is no way out without some sort of trap alarm or even a sort of key that prevents the traps from operating. I'm still trying to find a way, but it's just a way to kill time until I decide to run the tunnels and die." He hesitated. He had not thought the matter through to its necessary end like this before. He looked away from the woman and spoke in a quiet voice. "Those who die dishonored never see Valhal."

Aneala gave Egil a vigorous slap on the shoulder. "Cheer up! Talk not of death and this Valhal. I, too, have maps and I have figured out the floor traps." She unfolded a series of carefully drawn maps. "See, I have mapped each of the marked tunnels to the first trap or beyond. *I* know the traps. *You* can read the words that say where the tunnels go." She looked at Egil narrowly. "Can't you? That is what the words say, is it not?"

Egil smiled faintly and nodded.

"Good. Then if we work as partners, we learn faster, no?"

"Perhaps."

"That sly one, that Magnus, he took you through the tunnels. He showed you the traps, did he not?"

"Some traps."

"Good, good. You will describe them to me, I will figure them out, and then we will go."

"I've only started figuring out the traps I've seen—"

"No worries! I have, as I said, figured out the floor traps. It will not take long to learn the others, once I know what they are like. At this I am very good. It is part of my hobby. It is not only this civilization that has protected its treasures with traps."

So Egil told her what he had seen, and she let him copy details from her maps, but the meeting left him with an uneasy feeling. If they escaped as partners, who would make the first, most dangerous trip down a tunnel? How would they know how far they had to go? What kind of supplies would they need? Egil knew Starker IV's weather was more treacherous than its people. Most important, did Aneala really know the traps as well as she said she did?

For a week and a half they shared information. Then, a day after he translated for her the words that told where each of the main tunnels led, Watchers brought her body into the great hall. She had not seen this stake trap soon enough to catch an edge. Egil looked at the bloodied body as the Watchers readied it for the pyre and cursed Aneala for her impatience and dishonesty. He cursed himself for even dreaming he could outwit traps that had successfully defended the Watchers for almost two thousand years.

CHAPTER 3

On what was, by Egil's best estimate, 34 Koort, Frigdis drew him away from the table at nightmeal and into a narrow tunnel. Her usually serene face was taut and her movements abrupt. She looked up at him earnestly and took a deep breath.

"Egil"—she looked down at the floor—"in spite of our— we need—" She looked up at him. "You are familiar with the Seeing. You spoke sometimes during your long healing, so we know your mother and sister are Ones-Who-See. Sybils, your people call them."

Egil nodded. His mind raced, trying to figure out what a Seeing on an alien world could have to do with him.

"We observe the Upper World regularly," Frigdis went on. "For our own protection, we must know what the Gharr do. Well . . . " She sighed and shook her head. "We had hoped not to involve you, an outsider, in this, but we can delay no longer and the matter does involve you in a way, through your friend, the Halarek, and his clan enemy, the Duke of Harlan. We invite you to come, to share a Seeing with us."

Frigdis tentatively tugged at Egil's sleeve to encourage him to follow her along the tunnel. Egil, his curiosity pricked, followed willingly.

Frigdis continued. "The godi and his advisers (I am one) have foreseen House Harlan and its Old Party allies driving the Gild away, and that would lead to such desperation and violence as to end the rule of law in the Upper World entirely. Such would end our communities, too."

Egil jerked away from her hand, anger rising in him like a flood tide. When he spoke, his voice was low and taut. "How can my friend be 'involved' in what sounds like the end of civilized life here? He's not that sort of person!"

Frigdis's voice was low, too, and sounded embarrassed. "I—I thought it might ease you to see your friend. No." She put up a hand to stop an outburst from Egil. "Don't try to deny it. You've been tight as a harp string for weeks. You can actually see him if you come." She looked at the floor again. "I—I really thought it would ease your mind, the Seeing."

"Ease me? To see how his life goes when I can't be there? How can it ease me to see how I've failed him?"

"It was through no act of yours that you lived and dead you would have been no value to him. It was no act of yours gave you back your hands; you would have been of no value to him without them, either."

"I know that. *You* know there are no excuses for breaking oath but insanity or death. I'm neither insane nor dead. I don't want to see him. I hurt enough without that."

"Do you care nothing about what happens to him and the Gharr?"

"I care what happens to Karne. As for the rest of them . . . The Gharr are not—gentle—with outsiders." He turned away.

Frigdis laid her hand on his arm again. "No. Don't leave." Her quiet, pleading voice stopped him. "We are of the same blood and we believe in the same gods. We understand your sense of honor and the pain it is causing you. Perhaps there is a way to redeem it, but only if you come to the Seeing."

Egil hesitated. Why should he help these people? They had demolished his dreams and left him to live the rest of his life in dishonor and uselessness. These were the people who set and tended traps that killed innocent travelers. These were the people who brought Aneala's gory and mutilated body as an example to the other guests. Yet, even as he resisted Frigdis's pressure, he reminded himself that what the Watchers did, they did to protect themselves from the rapacious lords of Starker IV. All the Viking kind understood survival. And they *had* healed his hands, mostly. He could afford to show gratitude, even at the cost of a little pain, seeing Karne, left alone to fight his enemies by rules he no longer remembered.

"Egil?" Frigdis looked worried. "Please come?"

Egil looked down at her. He could not see how anything could ease his own intolerable situation, nor could he see how Karne could be involved in any planetary disaster. On the other hand, going with Frigdis could not make matters worse. "I'll come," he said.

He followed her to a small room off a narrow tunnel. The roof here was low, the walls rough-cut, and the light not as bright as in the main tunnels and halls. A close look around the room revealed no viewing equipment, no tri-d, no vids, no screen. How could they show him anything without equipment? Seeing was a woman's gift.

The godi and two Watchers he did not know stood beside a small table with a top of crystal laced with fine gold wires. The godi's fingers trailed absently across the crystal surface. He looked up as Egil came to stand opposite him. "We have decided," he said, "my advisers and I, to show you"—he pointed to the table—"what the other guests know nothing of." He then indicated the other men in turn with a jerk of his head. "My housecarls, Arne and Floki."

Arne was lean and sharp-boned, with a square jaw and coarse blond hair. Floki was shorter, stouter, and dark. The red veins of his prominent nose suggested he liked beer or ale far too well.

"They are also among the best of our Seers," the godi went on, "which is why they are here. You are here because you have made more than clear that your honor and the keeping of oaths are both extremely important to you."

Egil's mind began casting around for a reason for this to be important now, since his demand for the right to satisfy the claims of his honor had fallen on deaf ears earlier.

The godi continued. "We know that among your people, only women practice the Gift of Seeing. Here all do. During the terrible early years when our ancestors tried to live on the surface here, the savage winters forced our forebears into a sort of hibernation during the coldest times. They retreated into their minds and, led by sybils, slowly learned to See the present, the past, and, sometimes, the future." The godi looked at the aimless pattern his fingers were tracing on the tabletop. "As you know, to see at times the future has always been the gift of the Viking kind, in one degree or another. But that gift is fickle, coming and going as it pleases." The godi looked up and met Egil's eyes. "We control the Gift here, and not it us. Perhaps that is in part a mutation induced by the machines that aided that winter semihibernation. Perhaps not."

He certainly takes long enough to get to the point, Egil thought. *But that's a characteristic of politicians everywhere, I guess.*

The godi continued. "Your friend, as Frigdis probably told you, is a key to the disaster that will soon strike Starker IV unless someone prevents it. He is safe, as we've told you, for a time." The godi laughed grimly. "At the moment he is, of course, confined to his manor by winter, but he took fierce vengeance on Harlan first. He also spent a lot of money searching for you."

Egil flung back his head and straightened his shoulders. "Hearing what's happened, even Seeing it, whether for your benefit or mine, won't satisfy my oath."

The godi grimaced ruefully. "That I know. Perhaps we can aid you in the partial keeping of that oath, but there is a necessary formality here: You must swear to reveal to no one, ever, our presence or what you See here before we can show you anything."

Egil wondered what use such an oath could be. The godi had made quite clear, aided by Magnus's "tour," that there was no way out, had never been, would never be. Egil shrugged. "Why swear?"

"It is a formality. What is Seen is secret until what was observed is carefully analyzed, to separate symbol from real, for instance. Then the community learns what we have Seen. We have never in all our history given a Seeing without such a swearing." The godi shrugged. "If the oath is no use, it is also no harm."

That sounded reasonable enough. Egil understood custom and tradition very well. He also knew he had to be very careful, because the oaths of the Viking kind often held concealed traps that only a very clever man could later escape. On the other hand, the sybils of Balder held their most important Seeings in secret, perhaps for similar reasons of specialized interpretation.

He looked down at the gleaming surface of the crystal table. It had been cut and shaped and polished with consummate workmanship. For a moment he thought he saw movement on its surface, though what he should have seen was the red-brown of the floor. He shook his head. An illusion, brought on by thinking too much of sybils and Seeing.

The godi extended his right arm, turning it so the broad gold arm ring, the symbol of a godi's rights and power, faced Egil with its broadest part. One placed a hand on a godi's ring to make oath.

Egil wondered if the ring had been temple-blessed. He decided that in his present situation it did not matter. He had nothing to lose and at least a glimpse of Karne's life to gain. There would be no problem keeping this meeting secret from the other guests and he had no chance of ever again seeing anyone from the Upper World, so he could never reveal the Watchers' presence. He laid his hand on the ring.

"I swear by the ring, and by Heimdal, who is my special protector, that I will never reveal either the presence of the people called the Watchers or what I see here to any living being." He stepped back. "Is that sufficient?"

The godi bent his head in agreement. "You must touch the table with your hands. This allows us to extend the Sight to you. It also magnifies the power in each of us."

The group made a circle around the table, with Arne on one side of Egil and Frigdis on the other. Egil noticed the gold, thumb-sized indentations all around its rim.

"Put each thumb in a gold spot," the godi ordered, "and concentrate, Egil Odinsson, on the face of your friend. The rest of us will bring his picture to you. We will begin with what happened while you were healing. Now, concentrate."

Egil reminded himself to tell the godi later that Balder had given up naming children after their fathers in the old way, then closed his eyes and imagined Karne's angular brown face, dark brown hair, and golden eyes.

"Nay," Frigdis whispered, "you cannot close your eyes. What can you see with your eyes closed? Look at the table."

Egil obeyed. At first he saw only the vague movement he had seen before, then the motion coalesced into Karne's familiar features and then into Karne standing in a clear box in a large circular room, something like a theater. People in House colors and in the sark and hosen of Freemen filled the room.

Egil jerked his hands away from the table. "You didn't say he was safe because he was in prison!"

The picture in the table blurred and began to wobble.

"You assume we have less honor than you." The godi's voice was ice. "We show you the past. We *told* you that. Later the present. This happened while you were still at the Place of Leaving."

"We have no reason to shade truth," Arne added. "He is your friend and we do this as favor to you. Karne Halarek is not the man of interest to us at the moment."

"You knew he was of interest to me!" Egil flared. "You used—"

"Shut your mouth and listen!" Frigdis snapped. She tugged Egil back to the edge of the crystal, giving his knuckles a sharp rap on the edge in the process. "It takes much concentration to bring sound as well as sight to a non-sybil and you are hindering us!"

"I'm sorry." Egil made himself relax.

The colors and movements within the table again solidified into people and furnishings. Rows upon rows of benches, divided into wedges by aisles, filled with men.

Nine long tables sat directly on the central floor over about half the circle. Men in House colors sat at several of these tables, men in the same colors sat on the benches behind them, and the clear box, empty, sat beside one of them. Faint at first, then louder, came the murmur of a large crowd.

The scene begins a few minutes earlier this time, Egil thought, or later. Either they really can see distant places or this table is a very clever projection screen.

He bent a little closer. If the table had some kind of mechanical projection, it was too minute for him to see the mechanism. Perhaps the tiny gold wires had something to do with it.

Council soldiers guided Karne Halarek through a cluster of men in the colors of House Odonnel and House Kingsland and down the long aisle to the Halarek prep table, where they forced him into the clear box.

Egil tightened in outrage. The Lharr Halarek, confined like a criminal, and in front of all the lords of the Nine, too! Egil had not been long on Starker IV before learning how important reputation and public image were among the Families. This sort of confinement was an insult of the worst kind.

One of the soldiers pulled his stunner, pointed it at Karne, and fired.

Egil drew a harsh breath and shut his eyes.

"Watch, you, son of Odin."

Egil reluctantly opened his eyes.

The sides of the box had flushed faintly pink. Karne smiled thinly at the soldier, who smiled shyly back, waved, and then marched out of the chamber. Two Council men stayed behind to guard the door of the box.

The scene in the crystal vanished for a moment.

"Half-an-hour wait," Floki explained. "We're editing."

• • •

In the Council chamber, Richard Harlan strode down the aisle to the Halarek section and knelt at the Larga's side. Karne sprang to the door of the box. The two Council soldiers moved together, facing Richard and blocking Karne. Richard lifted the Larga's hand to his forehead in the Gharr gesture of deepest respect. The Larga jerked her hand away. Richard laughed and stood. His voice came to Egil thinned and blurry.

"Don't be angry, my lady. When today's meeting is over and its issues settled, our Houses will no longer be at war with each other. The feud will be ended. I hope this pleases you and the Lady Kathryn. Please express my admiration to her and tell her I hope to tell her myself in person soon."

The Larga paled. Beside the von Schuss table, Nik von Schuss sprang to his feet. Only the baron's hand restrained him.

Egil ground his teeth. "No!" he said with great force.

Richard laughed, bowed to the Larga with practiced grace, threw a triumphant look at Karne, a speculative one at Nik, and walked across the open side of the Nine's half-circle to the Harlan prep table.

The Larga spun toward Karne, her face still pale. "Never," she whispered. "I'll never let him have Kathryn."

"Don't let him see how effective he was, Lady Mother," Karne said very quietly. "We've given the bastard too much satisfaction as it is."

Just then, with a blare of ceremonial trumpets, the Marquis of Gormsby entered with a guard of Council soldiers.

Frigdis broke her grip on Egil's hand. She rested her open hands on the table and rolled her head from shoulder to back to other shoulder to front and around again. "I have not concentrated so much in long and long," she said. "Seeing is believing, as the ancients said, but now you have Seen the Halarek alive I would prefer to summarize what happened and skip on to the end of the meeting, to Council sentence. Does that suit you"—she looked at Egil—"or the rest of you?"

"Council sentence for whom?" Egil heard the sharp edge on his question.

Frigdis rolled her head again, rotated her shoulders a few times, then looked up at Egil with a wry smile. "You sound like you doubt the honor of the lords of the Nine Families." She gave a snort of derision. "What honor have they? Godi, shall we go on?"

The godi smiled faintly. "You're the storyteller."

Egil noticed that they had not answered his question.

Frigdis turned and braced herself carefully against the edge of the table. The other Watchers settled into relaxed positions on the floor and Egil followed suit. "There were parliamentary squabbles over the order of business, the Harlan trusteeship, the so-important Gild report." Frigdis glanced at Egil. "The Gild report, if you'll remember, had to do with whether or not House Harlan, in the person of the late duke, had anything to do with the many assassination attempts on Karne Halarek while he was on Gildships."

Egil nodded. He remembered. A letter from Karne recounting his difficulties aboard the Gildship had been Egil's introduction to the savagery of politics and clan feud of Starker IV.

Frigdis took a deep breath and looked off at the far wall, as if seeing the story there. "The chairman ordered the vote on the trusteeship, because the Gild report had not yet come." Frigdis's voice dropped lower and became more intense. "And the Gild report had not yet come because the chairman had ordered Council soldiers to keep the Gild delegation from entering. The Gild! The Gildsmen threatened to put Starker IV under indefinite embargo."

Egil drew in a sharp breath.

Frigdis looked at him approvingly. "I see you understand what an embargo would mean. To the Gharr, at least." She changed position slightly. "The Gild reported irrefutable evidence that Harlan tried many times to kill young Halarek, handed over the evidence, including photos, and left. Very shortly thereafter, Harlan tried to knife Lord Karne. The Larga shoved her son out of the way and took the knife herself."

"No," Egil whispered. He thought of the tiny golden woman, with all her charm, her beauty, her wit, her vanity, and most of all, her will of iron, a will that had held the Nine at bay until Karne could reach Starker IV. She was dead. Karne's chief source of knowledge about surviving in Gharr politics was dead. Egil shook his head. "What will Karne do without her? He's an innocent among butchers here."

"He's learning fast," the godi said dryly. "He took seven holdings from Harlan vassals before the storms came."

Floki laughed harshly. "To make matters worse for the 'butchers' of the Nine, the Freemen stripped the Families of the chairmanship, sentenced Richard Harlan to nine years solitary at Breven, and gave the trusteeship to Harlan's vassals."

Egil whistled low. "So much for House Harlan. It will be thirty tiny fiefdoms before Richard gets out." He looked at the godi. "But what about Karne?"

"Council, meaning the Freemen and minor Houses, named him head-of-House."

Egil shook his head, as if shaking would settle all the bits and pieces of what he had just heard and seen into one understandable whole. The Larga was dead, murdered. Richard was locked up for a long time, as time went for a lord of the Nine. Freemen now chaired Council. Karne was head-of-House and taking vengeance. Vengeance, at least, was something Egil understood very well, though on Balder in recent centuries such matters were usually settled by the Lawspeaker or by *holmganga* instead of with feud.

For a short time, silence filled the room. Then the godi stretched and arched his back.

"It's tiring work, especially bringing up sound. But you have seen that young Halarek is quite safe, for the moment."

Egil looked at the Watchers one by one. " 'At the moment'? Why only 'at the moment'? Richard's locked up. By the time he gets out, he won't have a loyal vassal left. And Frigdis spoke of a coming disaster, but the Larga is already dead. What do you know that you aren't saying?"

The Watchers looked at each other and the godi nodded. Frigdis licked her lips and glanced sidelong at the table before she spoke.

"Richard Harlan will escape Breven sometime in the spring." Frigdis paused and glanced at the others as if holding a silent consultation. "Halarek cannot yet withstand him, because the young Lharr is too inexperienced and too long away from Gharr ways. Harlan and his allies will return Starker IV to barbarism, which will cause the Gild to withdraw, which will destroy us and the Upper World, too."

CHAPTER 4

Egil gulped and stood stock still. "The Gild," he finally managed to croak, "the Gild supplies you?"

The godi gave a short bark of a laugh. "Son, how rich do you think the subterranean reaches of a mineral-poor world are? Of course the Gild supplies us—breeder reactor parts and fuel, hydroponics chemicals, fabrics, seed, electronic goods we cannot make ourselves from materials here—basic things."

"Wait a minute." Egil took a quick turn around the room. "The Gild knows about you but the Gharr don't?"

Arne and Floki both nodded.

"But how can that be?" Egil's tone was plaintive.

Floki shrugged. "Rigid tradition on both sides." He collapsed gracefully to the floor, tailor fashion, talking as he sat. "The Gild stands by its absolute neutrality. It prides itself in interfering in no way in any business but its own. If you remember, after those assassination attempts, the Gild decreed that it would carry no more members of the Nine anywhere, because one of the Nine had brought a feud aboard a Gildship and such feuds could damage the Gild's reputation by damaging its passengers or its goods. As for the Gharr, the nobility has very rigid beliefs: They believe they know everything about their world and their society that they need to know. It has always been that way when a powerful upper class controls a society's government and its military." Floki's voice shifted to a high and haughty tone. " 'We've got it all and we're not going to share.' "

Arne snickered, then sobered. "As a consequence, there's a lot about this world that the Gharr don't know."

"Like?"

"Us."

"So you spy on the Upper World to keep the Gild here?" Egil looked at each of the Watchers.

"Without the Gild, we don't survive," the godi said.

Arne steepled his fingers and stared down at the tips. "You can't begin to imagine how terrible life was in the first years after the crash. What this world had in resources and food was all there was. More than half the crash survivors died the first winter, from the cold. Half the rest died over the next five years."

"By the second generation, however," Floki added, "our forebears had galactic communication again. They contacted the Gild and the Gild came. We traded orak stone for goods for a couple centuries."

Arne nodded vigorously. "Still a very valuable trade item—"

Floki gave him a dark look and Arne shut his mouth ostentatiously. Floki continued. "The Gild offered to call a ship from Balder, but we had invested too much work and pain and grief in this world by that time." He glanced at Egil. "The Gild returned every year or two, until the Gharr settlement ships came. The communities asked the Gild to skip two summers so as not to reveal they already traded here, because we didn't know what sort of neighbors the Gharr would be." Floki sobered and stared at the rough‘red floor. "We were right to suspect the neighbors. They were, still are, a ruthless bunch of bandits."

The godi shook himself and glanced at the other Watchers. "We've wandered far from the subject, people."

Arne looked over at the godi, then at Egil, then shrugged. "It's clear to you now why the Gild must stay, Egil?" When Egil nodded, Arne continued. "House Harlan and House Halarek between them control the future of this world. Not by their wealth and political power do they have this control, because the gods know Halarek has precious little of either right now, but because their feud threatens the Gild's stay here. So we have watched them since the feud began."

Egil nodded.

Floki took up the explanation. "We have Seen Richard escape Breven and lead his House to control of Council and therefore of Starker IV. His Family will make this a world where robbery, torture, endless clan wars, famine, and slavery are the usual conditions. Perhaps you think the Gharr live that way now, but now there is at least the pretense of law and Council control—"

The godi cut Floki off with a slice of his hand, then gave Egil a long, considering look. He took a deep breath. "Richard Harlan is a leader of great charisma and skill. The Council defeated his bid for power this time because he, in his arrogant overconfidence, made illegal grabs for Halarek. House Halarek is not now strong enough nor the young Lharr wise enough in the ways of this world to withstand Harlan long, but the young Lharr is the only continuing opposition the duke has. If the duke escapes and defeats Halarek, the Gild will soon leave. It has never risked its assets on a world controlled by robbers or petty dictators. It has never needed to. It has always maintained a strict neutrality, even here among the outer worlds, because the worlds need the Gild. *It* doesn't need *them*." Then he added, as an afterthought, "In fact, most of the outer worlds adopted civilized forms of government primarily to get the Gild to come."

The godi straightened, wiped the palms of his hands against his hosen, then met Egil's eyes with intimidating directness. "We want you to capture Richard Harlan and return him safely to Breven before he can do any damage."

Egil's heart leaped. Richard Harlan! A chance for the vengeance Richard Harlan so thoroughly deserved! The godi was offering him a chance at Harlan! "Of course I will. Did you think for a moment that I'd refuse?" Incredulity made his voice crack on the high notes.

"I thought it very likely," the godi answered dryly, "when you learned the conditions."

Only then did Egil's racing mind hear the phrase "return him safely to Breven." His brain screamed at him, *Fool! Fool! Fool! You jumped at the bait too soon! You've let him box you in.*

For a moment Egil's anger turned against the godi, but the godi had only been playing by rules Egil understood well. He had just been cleverer.

The godi was watching him and Egil knew the man was aware of the rat-in-a-trap struggling of Egil's thoughts. He even waited for Egil to get his anger back under control before he continued. "It never occurred to me you would promise to capture Harlan without even asking the conditions. Is everyone on Balder so careless? Well, no matter. A promise is not an oath, but it is well along the way. You cannot in all honor now turn away from formalizing your promise." And before Egil had the wits to ask anything more, the godi had brushed past him and left.

Egil returned to his room. Hours later, he was still on the edge of his bed, cursing his own stupidity. He should have suspected at once the Watchers' reasons for showing him Karne's trial. *What better way to stir up a glory hound than to show something that increases his need for some powerful act of vengeance? The Larga's murder did that. Then they distract him and tempt him so he'll say something rash.*

As he thought about his disastrous evening, Egil became surer and surer that the wandering away from the subject and into the tale of the ships' survivors had been a disingenuous performance designed to increase the pressure of his curiosity and to lull his natural suspicion. He had fallen for the whole performance like a babe. He had promised impetuously, eagerly, to capture Richard, without a thought of what his opponent, the godi, would want in return. And a promise *was* only a step away from an oath. He had bound himself too tightly to wriggle out easily or honorably. Then he remembered he had already sworn to tell no living being of the Watchers' existence and kicked himself some more. That oath had not seemed to matter when life underground was all he had to look forward to.

Too late he remembered what the Lawspeaker had said

many times: "*Always* consider every *possible* aspect of an oath, not just the probable aspects." *And I didn't. I didn't! He reeled me in like a spider a fly!* This *is where my dreams of glory take me*.

In his innermost heart Egil admitted that, when the godi offered him the chance to take Richard, he had seen himself avenging the beautiful and once-powerful woman struck down so foully in the midst of her jeering enemies, perhaps winning her beautiful daughter to wife. Such stories made songs that lived a thousand years.

Now it was "night" in his bedroom, and the boyhood dream seemed overblown and silly. Such stories made fools! Egil rested his head in his hands. *My grandfather and father founded and expanded a great merchant empire. Hadd opened Canopia to trade after many had tried for two hundred years and failed. Hring was inventing improvements on starship guidance systems before he was twenty. Einar was a vice-admiral at thirty. Solveig is a noted sybil, as is Mother. Even Donner and Kenner are better than me, because they're brilliant scholars. And then there's me. I was going to be a harper and skald but didn't have the voice for it. Then I was going to be a famous painter and didn't have quite enough talent for that. I came here to be a war hero.* Egil gave a harsh, bitter bark of a laugh. "Cattle die and kinsmen die, and even you yourself will die, but fame, for the man that wins it, will never die."

Fame. Respect. Egil slumped lower until his forehead was almost on his knees. *What do I do now? By the Hammer! Must I always be the runt of the Olafsson litter?*

Long hours of shame, frustration, and despair followed. The worst of Egil's inner darkness lifted when he thought of the crystal table and the Seeing. Perhaps he could lessen the damage he had done with his rash promise. Return Harlan alive? What kind of vengeance was that?

Egil thought carefully. It was legal and acceptable, at least on Balder, to squirm out of oaths through any verbal or logical hole the oath presented. If Egil were lucky, and if he had even a little of his mother's talent, perhaps he could See the future, too, and thus gain some small advantage in his fated agreement with the godi. If the godi wanted Harlan, then surely the god must be taking a hand, so Egil need not break his oath to Karne. Heimdal did not want Egil to die an oath-breaker. Perhaps he would also help Egil See.

At an hour the chrono on his bedroom wall said was very early, Egil slipped out of his room. He kept telling himself that if he had even a little of the Olafsson Gift and were lucky, he had a slight chance of Seeing, too.

The room with the crystal table was easier to find than he had dared hope and there was no guard at the door to the room. The god's hand again. Egil peeped through a crack in the door. No guard inside, either. Egil took one step into the room. No alarm went off. He approached the crystal table. It gleamed in the subdued light of the room. He could not see even the vague movement he had seen in it before. He rested his hands on the edge of the table and stared down at the polished surface. Only the women were sybils. On all Balder, only women had ever been sybils. Was it custom only, or was there a biological reason? Egil asked Heimdal to help him, then focused on the center of the table.

He thought of Karne. He thought of him with great determination. The stone floor below the table's edge mocked him. The floor was smooth there, polished by the toes of users for hundreds of years, and solid beyond the power of whatever Gift he might have. Egil strained, willing something, anything, to come up in the surface. He saw only the gold-laced crystal and the shiny floor. Sweat trickled into his eyes. His thumb joints ached with the pressure on them. He began losing hope.

Suddenly, faintly, a crowd in festive clothes floated up in the glass. Slowly, as the image became stronger, Egil recognized the Great Hall at Ontar manor. Triumph surged through Egil and the picture vanished. Fiercely Egil suppressed the triumph and summoned all his concentration again. The Hall again swam up out of the crystal, hazy with incense and torch smoke, and distant as if he were watching from along the ceiling. The Hall was jammed with people in gay party colors. The torches flared along the walls. Banners in Halarek blue and green floated from the upper gallery.

"The banners have no black streamers," Egil muttered to himself. "At least it's not Karne's wake."

It was hard for him to decide what was happening, for he heard nothing and the image wavered like smoke the moment his attention lessened. A large group of people moved toward the head of the room. Karne stepped out of the group and onto the dais there. Karne's clenched fist shot above his head. The crowd leaped and waved kerchiefs and scarves. Though he could hear nothing, Egil knew from the previous ceremony that they were shouting, "Halarek lives! Halarek lives!"

Exultation wiped out Egil's concentration and the picture. "I can do it! I can do it!" He sagged against the table, sweating and drained. "Heimdal! My thanks!" he said. Then, "I'm so tired!" He remembered Frigdis's weariness after the Council viewing. Exultation surged again. "I have the Sight!"

His legs too tired to support him longer, Egil sat abruptly on the floor. He braced his elbows on his knees and rested his head in his hands. He realized he must have dozed off only when he heard bootheels snap against the floor near him. Egil jerked upright guiltily and looked up. The owner of the boots was the godi.

Not only am I in the viewing room without permission, but I shouted so everyone would know I'm here. Stupid!

"Were you successful?" the godi asked, crouching on his haunches so his eyes were on a level with Egil's.

"Successful?" Egil stalled, hoping to hide his confusion: The godi was not angry, as Egil had been sure he would be.

The godi laughed. "There's only one reason for anyone to come into this room, son, and that's to See. Besides, someone heard you shout, 'I have the Sight!' We didn't know for sure if you had the Gift, so we watched."

Tricked again! Egil was surprised at the bitterness that trickery stirred up in him. Yet the bait of freedom still dangled silently in front of him, like a deer leg in front of a hungry Zinn bear. He could not risk losing a chance at that bait by showing the godi his anger and bitterness at the trickery. Could he win the freedom to pursue Harlan at all, or was that, too, a trick? The Viking kind was adept at such tricks. He had played some of them himself.

Egil hoped his voice came out level and unconcerned. "What difference does it make to you?"

The godi studied Egil's face. "If you take our oath and you don't have the Gift, we must teach it to you with drugs and dreams. To succeed against Richard of Harlan, who knows this world and who will have armed men with him, you must have the Sight. It will be your only advantage."

"Why don't you just read my mind?"

"We told you when you first came and I tell you now again, we don't enter the minds of others. Such use is dangerous and divisive, so it was banned at the beginning. That means the skills to use it have never been developed, won't ever be. Can you imagine a close, crowded community such as ours, with not even the privacy of the mind left?" The godi stood. "Enough. Time grows short. Shorter if you have not the Seeing. Do you?"

"Aye, but it was fuzzy and dim and faded too quickly." Egil got wearily to his feet. He felt defeated and outguessed and cornered.

"Show me," said the godi.

"Show you?"

"Yes. Come." The godi motioned impatiently toward the table.

Karne stood on the dais. The image was clearer now, for Egil could recognize the full-sleeved tan shirt and Halarek blue vest, the cape, and the fur-trimmed trousers Karne wore as traditional Halarek ceremonial clothes. Karne had worn them at his ceremony of fealty. Karne's clenched fist shot above his head.

His coming of age! By all the gods, it's Karne's coming of age and I've seen it!

Egil's emotion wiped out the picture again. This time he let the exultation sweep through him and die away at its own pace.

"*Was* this Halarek's coming of age?" he finally asked.

The godi nodded. "As we told you, Lord Karne has been of age for months. It's deepest winter in the Upper World now." He moved back from the table. "You have the Seeing, and at a reasonable strength for one untrained. Your link of friendship and blood brotherhood makes Halarek easier for you to See. We can teach you some things and others, such as how to tell past from present from future, you will just know. But we can't teach you until we have your oath concerning Harlan."

"You really apply the pressure, don't you? I can see my closest friend only if I do what you ask."

The godi's face was grim. "We do what we must to survive. Does your friendship or blood brotherhood apply no pressure? Does your honor apply no pressure?" The godi's voice was harsh with his impatience. "We *must* stop Harlan and one of *us* would not survive Above. We have not known weather for two thousand years. You are our only hope. Yet we know the urge for blood vengeance, and we also know Harlan could not do the fighting and lovemaking necessary in the next few years without his hands."

Egil's laugh had a bitter edge. He held up his hands. "I lost these Above. What makes you think I can survive?"

"We'll train you to survive by mind-link with a Runner."

Egil stiffened. "You said entering the minds of others was forbidden."

The godi nodded. "That's exactly what I said. We don't enter the Runner's mind. He has offered the information in his memory for a—consideration—and the information will come to you through a library machine, something we've used since the crash to preserve memories and stories. You will reexperience the Runner's memories. It's painless and effortless, I assure you, and takes much less time and is far more efficient than transferring the information either by voice or in writing."

"And if I take this oath, I get my freedom and Karne's enemy?"

"You get your freedom and Karne's enemy. To bring to Council or to Breven, safe and alive."

That was too much. "Safe?" Egil roared, his frustration and shame getting the better of him. "That's not vengeance! What kind of mewling descendants of Odin are you here?"

A muscle in the godi's cheek jumped, but he did not even raise his voice. "It must be so, though why I may not tell you, because that would alter the future even more than our interference here. That is the condition: You get your freedom; Richard Harlan lives undamaged. If he does not, we'll snatch you back here, wipe the survival knowledge from your brain, and keep you here the rest of your life."

The godi turned to leave the room, then stopped and looked back over his shoulder. "Ordinarily we use the wiping process only on violent Runners, because they are a danger to us unless their memories are altered. Among our kind, the wipe often takes the Gift, too. Think carefully before you make oath, Egil Odinsson. You have three days." The godi walked out the door.

Three days.

Egil sat down again, heavily. He felt as if he had been standing on a sand cliff and all the sand had suddenly been cut from under his feet. He put his head in his hands.

Three days. If I refuse to take the oath, I stay here forever or I die in the tunnels and self-murder is dishonor, too. If I do take the oath, I cannot take my revenge on Harlan. If I break oath with the Watchers, not only am I dishonored, but I'll be snatched back here and have my memory wiped.

He looked blindly toward the Upper World and sky above that. "My god! Just this morning I thought you were handing me some luck! Why can't you arrange some easy choices?"

CHAPTER 5

Egil paced and thought for hours. He swam in the long tamed river the Watchers called a pool and thought. He sat in his darkened room and thought, then he walked to the edge of the first traps and looked down the long stone corridor to where the light faded to gray and then quit. He had sworn vengeance. Now he realized the hands would not be enough. Nothing less than Harlan's death would do. Harlan had murdered the Larga; he had destroyed Egil's hands; his treacheries against Karne were too many to count. On the other hand, Egil knew if he could not get out of the tunnels of the Watchers, he could not kill Harlan. If the Watchers let him out, it would be to *not* kill Harlan. Dishonor either way. If he ran a tunnel and died, at least that way his dishonor would be secret. But self-murder was also dishonor. And the gods would know what he had done and would close him off from Valhal and the company of fighting and drinking companions forever.

Egil turned from the tunnel in despair. Not today. He would not run a tunnel today. He would not run a tunnel until he felt entirely sure no other solution was possible. Egil's feet scuffed a narrow trail in the thin dust along the wall. The dust had a thin, dry smell. Richard Harlan was a danger to Karne Halarek and his House every moment he lived. Egil flexed his fingers, which still were not back to normal. The weakness of his hands would only make Harlan's death slower, not less certain. Harlan might be a master duelist, but Egil was a master at Drinn.

But if he killed Harlan, he would be brought back here forever.

Egil stopped, his eyes staring blindly at the gray stone floor. Karne could not know Harlan was going to escape and by the time he learned of it, Harlan was certain to be safe at home or with allies. He himself was the only person who could get Harlan and if he killed Harlan, even accidentally, he was doomed to a life underground among strangers. Egil walked slowly back toward his quarters. He must keep his word to defend Karne. Therefore, he had no alternative to taking the godi's oath, accepting its consequences, and hoping Heimdal would send him luck.

Once he had made his decision, Egil found waiting until nightmeal difficult, but the godi was available for community business only after meals. Egil spent the wait preparing himself as if for a temple ceremony. He bathed. He braided his hair and combed the new beard. He put on the finest of the clothes the Watchers had given him and then added bracelets, arm rings, and amber finger rings. Too nervous to eat, Egil waited until the after-meal drinks had been poured, then strode up to the godi's high seat.

"I'll take your oath. I'll catch Richard of Harlan for you," he said in a tight voice. He reached his hand toward the godi's armring.

The godi nodded approval but did not lean forward so Egil could reach the ring. "Good. You did not dally. I had hoped you would not. However, the oath-taking must be done in the temple. Tomorrow morning we will do it, before the entire community."

Frigdis, standing slightly behind Egil, made a sudden, protesting movement. "That's too quick," she said.

The godi lowered his voice and spoke with a gentleness Egil had not heard before. "My dear, there is no time. You know there is no time."

After a long pause, Frigdis murmured, "No, of course there isn't. It was silly of me to protest. May I let the other communities know, though, that we've found someone who will do the work?"

The godi smiled faintly. "Of course, my dear. As soon as you like."

For a second, Egil wondered where these "other communities" were, then he wondered why he had never seen a connection between the godi and Frigdis before. But that was a small matter. The proposed oath would change his life, and for the worse.

"Gentlehom, what does this ceremony involve? What are you expecting me to do?"

"To swear to capture Harlan without killing him. No more. No less." The godi paused. "The temple ceremony allows many people to witness the oath, because the results of your hunt are vitally important to all of us. The ceremony will also give the extra power of the gods to the fulfilling of the oath." The godi glanced toward the tunnel where Frigdis had gone. "We do understand vengeance, though you may not now believe that. We think to make your vow easier to keep by having many witnesses."

Egil made a slight bow, as he would have to a godi at home, and went to his quarters. Frustration and despair tore at him. *The godi most definitely knows what he's doing. Now, after I kill Richard and the Watchers snatch me back, everyone in this community will look at me with contempt for breaking faith with them. No matter which oath I keep, I'm doomed to live out my life in disgrace and shame. No glory. No fame for the rightful killing of such a one. Not even the small fame of recognition for a ___ well done. No matter what I do now, I won't add to my family's glory. I can't be a part of it. I'll be a disgrace to them.*

Egil flopped onto his bed and threw his arm over his eyes. A disgrace. A shame. When he had had such grand dreams!

The night was long and black. Early in the morning, a young boy awakened him. Egil found rising almost more than he could manage. He had to bathe, to present himself clean before the gods, then dress in the same finery as the day before. He felt as though he stood in honey, which clung to his limbs and slowed every movement. He wished briefly he had ribbons to braid into his beard to make the dressing ritual complete.

When Egil finished, the boy handed him a hip-length cloak, red with braided trim of gripping beasts and kraken, and led him to the temple.

The temple was large, larger than any room Egil had seen among the Watchers. Across the room from the entry doors were three immense thrones. On the thrones sat three gods, giant human figures carved or molded from some substance with skin-like tones. Thor sat in the center throne. His red beard and hair bristled as if alive with the lightning he so often played with. He wore his iron gloves and Mjollnir, his huge hammer, lay across his lap. Odin sat to his right, his ravens on his shoulders, his one eye glaring balefully out across the room. Frey, god of love and marriage, sat cross-legged in his chair, beautiful, naked, and aroused. Between the gods and the worshippers stood an immense altar, large enough to take the sacrifice of a horse or even a ulek. High above the altar, on pulleys that at the moment held them close to the ceiling, hung rows and rows of hooks.

Egil stared up at them for a long time. Eight times nine, perhaps nine times nine hooks. Egil could not remember being in a temple that still had hooks. But this was a very old place and the Watchers were a very old people, cut off from changes in the rest of the galaxy. Perhaps they still held sacrifice here. There were tales from ancient times of the Great Feast, held once every nine years, when nine of each kind of living creature were sacrificed. Even humans. He shivered. Surely not.

The boy tugged at Egil's sleeve. Egil dipped until one knee touched the floor, a proper obeisance when one brought neither a petition for the gods nor gifts, then straightened and followed the boy toward the front of the hall. Others came forward with gifts of goods or meat, which they placed on the altar, then they lay briefly prostrate on the floor, murmuring their wishes and prayers. When Egil reached the front, all the supplicants stepped back.

From the entry came a blare of horns, and from behind Odin came the godi, bearing the temple's most holy armring on a golden tray. Men and women carrying flaming torches marched on both sides of him and formed a ring around the altar. They parted on the side toward the congregation, revealing the godi in the center of a ring of fire, then they continued to straighten the circle until they were lined up across the feet of the gods. All the gold and jewels on the figures flamed to life.

"Egil, son of Odin!" The godi's voice boomed through the chamber.

Egil stepped away from the boy guide. The tray had to have come with the ship, because Starker IV had no gold.

The godi handed the tray to one of his attendants and poured a libation of wine at the feet of each of the gods, murmuring prayers. As he watched, Egil began to hope. If the godi gave the oath to Egil Odinsson, Egil Olafsson could capture Richard and do with him as he liked without dishonor, for the oath would not by law apply to Egil Olafsson. Freedom *and* vengeance. Egil was glad he had not told the godi that on Balder, children no longer took their father's first name as their last name. That would be small repayment for the tricks the godi had played on him. Excitement swept through Egil and he struggled to suppress it. If it showed in his face or body's movements, the godi would suspect something. The godi was a clever man. He would track down the cause of Egil's excitement like a hound and like as not come close enough to the truth to stop Egil somehow from profiting from the godi's error.

"Egil, son of Odin, come to me!"

The godi's command ripped through Egil's thoughts and smashed the small hope growing there. The godi lifted the armring from the tray, raised it, and turned slowly with the ring held high so all could see, then gestured for Egil to join him on the gods' side of the altar. The godi extended the ring toward Egil and spoke in the cadence of the old lays.

> "Here is the oath ring, blessed by the gods,
> Brought now before you to testify truth."

The godi turned a little toward Egil, but not enough that the witnesses could not clearly hear his voice.

"Swear now before us, saving not back,
Lest from your reticence, ruin result."

The godi motioned for Egil to lay his hand on the ring. He looked at Egil, waiting.

There was still a tiny chance the godi's words would give Egil a hole to slip through. Egil bent his head meekly a moment. "This ceremony is new to me, gentlehom. Say you the words you want and I'll say them back."

The godi paused a moment, staring deep into Egil's eyes. Egil, not entirely trusting assurances that the Watchers read no minds, carefully kept his head clear of all thoughts of names or vengeance or Richard Harlan.

The godi lifted the ring a little higher. "Say, then, 'I, Egil, son of Odin, swear that I will capture Richard Harlan alive and neither kill him nor injure him so that he dies. I also swear that I will turn Richard Harlan over to Breven or to the World Council, so that no one else may kill him or injure him so that he dies."

Egil repeated the words carefully, exactly, clearly.

The godi has covered all the territory, he thought, heart sinking. There's no possibility of "accidentally" killing Harlan nor of giving him over to his enemies, who would kill him yet leave my hands clean. I should've expected no less from a man who has to know well the legal ways to escape a carelessly stated oath.

The godi set the ring on the tray again, which apparently ended the ceremony. Worshippers began streaming out the doors. The godi held Egil from joining them with a firm grip on his arm.

"A moment more of your time, Egil, son of Odin. We *do* understand vengeance, as I've told you before. Nine years in Breven is, to Harlan, a far worse punishment than any death or torment you could devise. Believe it now or learn it later, it's all the same." He gave Egil a mighty thump on the shoulder. "There's a great feast in the hall in your honor now. Let's eat."

Egil followed the godi out of the temple. There was always a feast after a temple ceremony and, from the offerings on the altar, there would be fresh meat on the table. Egil grinned, remembering the dismay of devout cadets from other worlds who were horrified that Balder sacrifices were either eaten by the worshippers or given to the poor.

"Fresh meat won't do carved gods any good," Egil had always told them. "You or me, now, or poor people who have neither hunters nor money . . . "

They usually failed to see the practicality of the arrangements, anyway, at least at first.

The feast was vast, the drinking that followed it intense, and the headache the next morning even more intense. The day after that, Egil's training in the ways of the Desert of Zinn and other wild places began. First, several tailors spent most of that day measuring Egil for survival clothes. Then came the lessons. For weeks came the lessons. From wake-up to daymeal, Egil lay in a small cubicle connected by wires through a library machine to a lanky Runner, absorbing at high speed knowledge of the edible or useful plants and animals and the poisonous or dangerous ones, of hiding places, of customs of the Runners that would protect him if he met them, of the habits of Dur cat, Zinn bear, musk cobra, and schlange lizard. He learned how best to cross rivers, how to judge the safety of ice, and what trees had the best bedding branches. By the time each daymeal time arrived, Egil felt as if his brain were full to bursting.

After every daymeal, Egil walked to the craft shops in the far corner of the settlement to be fitted for clothes and gear. The backpack he would take had to be custom-shaped to his back for comfort and maximum loadability. Since he had to be dressed both to survive the cold and to fit in with the Runners and "other wildlife," as Magnus put it, he could not have a step-in, all-weather survival suit such as he had had while he was with Karne at Ontar manor. He was to have waterproof and snowproof footgear, boots for hard walking, rain clothes, summer clothes, furs in parkas and trousers like those worn by the ancient migrants of Terra's Arctic. The quantity and variety suggested the Watchers expected a long chase.

If Egil's mornings were mind-numbing from the sheer volume of information he had to learn, the afternoon fittings were mind-numbingly boring. Not only must he stand still, still, still, he had no one to talk to but the tailor, who almost always had a mouthful of pins. The tailor made the garments by cutting roughs from the measurements he had made of Egil's body, then pinning and cutting the garment pieces to their final shape on Egil.

After the fittings came the training of his Gift, usually for several hours after nightmeal. He learned to concentrate on the surface of the crystal table and pull out images, first with the assistance of Frigdis and then without. His images were often fuzzy and there was no sound, but he quickly learned that One-Who-Sees "knew" which visions were the past, which the present, which the future. Within a few weeks, Egil could draw out images whenever he wished. In those practice Seeings, Egil Saw Karne take the small holdings of Jura, Lÿnn, Skabish, and Brassik. The storms of Uhl prevented a successful siege at Rhiz. Egil Saw Karne at Rhiz, half obscured by blowing snow, directing troops into transports back to Ontar. Karne had learned well the lesson of Farm 3, where his generals had left the men in the snow and cold until great numbers of them got frost fever.

Egil endured the tailor's fittings in martyred silence for more than a Gildweek before the standing still and the sweating and the lack of conversation shattered his resolve to be patient. At the moment his patience snapped, he had been standing for hours under a load of bear and ulek-hide, cold-weather outerwear, which, of course, had to be fitted over everything he would be likely to wear underneath. The warmth of the furs plus the warmth of the room was making him feel dizzy and faint.

"Why all this deep-cold gear? You expect me to chase this rat through the winter?" he demanded. "I've been through a winter here: And a spring, which nearly killed me." He rubbed his hands against each other, remembering, and again thanked the gods he had them back.

The tailor, who was ruthlessly sticking pattern pieces to Egil's clothing—and skin—with long pins, mumbled something around the pins in his mouth. It was entirely unintelligible.

Egil let out a big disgusted sigh and stared hard at the wall across from him. It was smoother than most of the walls in the settlement, perhaps because the tailor hung unfinished clothes there and fabrics that might snag or tear. At the corner where that wall met another was a full-length mirror. Egil could see the front half of himself at the moment, and the tangles of fabric and scraps and huge bobbins of thread on several of the tailor's worktables. For lack of anything better to do, Egil concentrated on the bright surface of the glass, practicing focusing his attention as if the glass were the godi's table.

Egil let his mind float. He saw the green of Balder, his family's airy glass house, and the cloudless blue sky above it. Slowly he let himself absorb the warmth and comfort of that faraway world. He felt the sun, heard his father's deep voice, the lighter musical voice of his mother, the boisterous laughter of his brothers and sister. It was the voices that told him this was not the mirror but his own memories, for he could not yet receive sound. He remembered the slowness of Solveig's learning to separate memory from Sight. He looked at the mirror again, consciously blocking the doors to memory. Perhaps it would help if he thought about his purpose, the reason why he was standing very still and sweating: All this discomfort would lead to the duke-designate in Harlan and that would lead to keeping faith with Karne.

At first the mirror only glinted back at him. Then dark shadows gathered, clustered, took shape. He saw a tiny, dim room that contained a narrow bed, a small desk, and a tall, narrow window. Excitement stirred in Egil. This was not Ontar. This was someplace new, a place he had never seen before. Because of his excitement, the room faded to faint gray shadows and it took several minutes to call the image back. This time it was sharper. The room contained a tall figure in the gray habit and hood of a Retreat House deacon or deaconess. Excitement stirred again at the back of Egil's mind. He squashed it immediately. The figure walked to the door and handed something to someone outside, then shut the door, sat down at the desk, and threw back the hood. The dark handsome face was Richard Harlan's.

Exultation wiped out the figure and the room and the shadows. Egil saw only the bright reflections in the mirror, but it was enough. Enough! He could See without the table! He could See someone with whom he had no ties of love. In his joy he must have moved, because the tailor jerked and cursed and stuck a bleeding finger into his mouth. The tailor thus disabled, Egil peeled himself out of the pattern pieces and sprang toward the door.

"That's all for the day. Sorry. Got to see Frigdis and the godi."

The tailor took his finger out in order to curse Egil more fluently. His words floated harmlessly down the tunnel on Egil's heels.

CHAPTER 6

Egil found Frigdis and Magnus in the room where he had first awakened, which he now thought of as the infirmary. They were sitting on a bench beside the black pool, reading. The good news rushed out before Egil was close enough to talk at normal volume.

"I can See! I can See!" he bellowed from across the room.

Magnus put down his book. Frigdis looked up from her knitting. "Ah," she said.

"Show us," Magnus said, rising from his chair.

The three went to the viewing room, where Egil explained that he had Seen in the tailor's mirror, then set his thumbs in the depressions in the table. He thought better of it and clasped his hands behind his back instead.

"I didn't need to touch the mirror," he explained.

He focused his eyes on the golden wires and thought of Karne. Almost at once Karne appeared, sitting in the manor library with Tane Orkonan, his secretary; a very thin, sharp-faced old man; and Kit. Egil assumed the old man was Karne's former secretary, who had left Ontar right before Egil's arrival. The group seemed to be discussing something very serious: Even the usually bouncy Kit was sitting quietly, hands folded gracefully in her lap. Then Egil noticed a tall, spare figure in the shadows behind Kit.

"The redoubtable Lady Agnes," he muttered. "Guardian of propriety and maidenly virtue. Must be a very serious matter if she can make Kit sit like a lady."

He tried to remember what sort of relative Lady Agnes was and gave up. His mind had been focused almost entirely on the feud during his time at Ontar. The images wavered and faded away as Egil's mental focus slipped.

Magnus gave Egil a resounding slap on the shoulder. "Good! Good! No hands, even."

Frigdis briefly touched his clasped hands. "Is this what you Saw in the mirror?" she asked. "This conference about a bride and a groom to bring heirs to House Halarek?"

"Is that what that was?" So Kit was to be married. Well, she was sixteen and old enough. Egil shook his head. "No, what I Saw was Richard at Breven."

Frigdis's eyes took on a glow. "Good, oh, good! You aren't limited by your blood tie." She smiled brilliantly. "Some are, you know, and we could have worked with that, but it would have been much harder. Bring back what you Saw."

Egil remembered the tiny room with its narrow bed and tried to call it up, but what came into the table was a small kitchen garden in early evening. A shadow moved by the garden wall and then the image faded from the table.

"That was not it, was it?" Magnus's question was really more of a statement.

"No, and I don't understand. I can see that room in my mind as well as if I'd been there."

"That is part of the training, too. We had not thought to get to it quite so soon." Frigdis did not look disappointed that the lesson would have to be changed.

"Learning to See a precise point in time can come later. You're ready for your test now," Magnus said.

Frigdis glanced at Magnus and shook her head disapprovingly. Magnus ignored her.

"The godi wants you to practice your skills Above before they are actually needed. Your hands are not up to full strength yet and will not be for two or three more months. It is very early spring in the Upper World, before the New Year's thaw, so we can learn your resistance to cold and how well your equipment protects you from it without great risk to you. As has been said, your hunt may be long. You must remember, we do not go Above much, so there may be flaws in our plans, items forgotten in centuries of repetition."

Egil's blood ran cold. He had not considered the Watchers' inexperience with the weather of the Upper World. He looked down at his hands. Would losing them again be another cost of his hunt? He remembered the pain and then the numbness. He forced those memories aside.

"—will be staying within fifty kilometers of a Place of Leaving this time," Magnus was saying, "so you can be rescued, if necessary. The test will begin the second morning from now." Magnus turned to leave.

"Magnus," Frigdis said warningly.

Magnus turned back with some irritation. "What more? You want me to explain the test completely?"

Frigdis shook her head a tiny bit.

"The Dur cat part, eh?" When she nodded, Magnus grimaced. "You're sure the godi won't be angry that I've stolen his prerogative?"

"The old godi would have been, perhaps, but not my brother."

Magnus looked up at Egil. "You *have* heard of the Dur cats?"

Egil nodded.

"The Dur cat is the real test. Inadequate equipment can always be modified or replaced. Dur cats are about the smartest and the most vicious animals ever discovered. Starker IV exported them as gladiatorial animals for centuries, then a combination of off-world breeding and a scarcity here ended the trade. They're almost knee-high, black, with six-centimeter claws in bright yellow sheaths. Other worlds know them almost exclusively for the 'killing rage' that does not end until the cat or every living creature within the cat's reach is dead. They are as the berserks are among us, only with fur."

Egil had seen the berserk rage in the Drinn ring and the ten men needed to hold the berserk until his rage died. Imagining such a rage in a large cat with very long claws was not comforting.

Magnus studied his fingers. "This rage is not a trait likely to promote survival in captivity, hence their rarity. Our berserks lasted in battle largely because their opponents felt they were under the hand of a god. This rage also explains why Dur cats were so 'entertaining' in gladiatorial contests, where weapons are carefully matched for 'fairness.' Claws and rage versus . . . " Magnus looked up at Egil. "Your test is to catch and tame, at least enough to handle, one of these cats. Such taming is possible. That's proven by the cats' long history as bodyguards and, sometimes, pets. You can look at this test as a trial run against a strong and wily opponent, Richard Harlan with four legs, so to say." Magnus's voice grew more intense. "You *must* consider it an important test, because if you fail to capture a cat, or fail to tame one after its capture, you will not be allowed to hunt the Harlan."

Egil held up his hands.

"Aye," Magnus conceded, "they are not to full strength. But time is short, and we had expected the healing to proceed faster. We do our best to prepare you for your hunt. The godi will explain whatever else you need to know tomorrow."

"But it *will* be very difficult," Frigdis added in a low voice. "There's a good chance you'll die in the attempt." She looked up with such sadness in her eyes that Egil's stomach turned over. "In this test we can give you aid in case of disaster. You will be beyond our help when you hunt Harlan."

"Breven itself is beyond our reach, but none of the Holdings are," Magnus added, "so get no ideas about escape. You know well now what it would be like to live as a Runner lives out there."

The Runners lived edge-of-starvation lives, hunted by animals and other Runners as well. Most of them did not survive.

Immediately after the talk with Magnus and Frigdis, Egil went over all his equipment, at least all the equipment now piled in his room waiting for use. He compared each piece to what he had learned from the Runners about the

Upper World and what he had learned, painfully, himself. It seemed adequate.

His instructions the next day, delivered by the godi, were brief and accompanied by none of the ceremony the Gharr would have given it: Egil had as long as was necessary to tame the cat or until the duke escaped Breven. If the cat were not manageable by that time, Egil would not again be allowed on the surface because the Watchers considered succeeding in taming a Dur cat the only proof that Egil had learned enough self-control to refrain from killing Harlan.

When the godi finished his instructions, Egil unleashed the anger he felt about this dangerous addition to his training, an anger that had been building since Magnus had told him of the test. "This was *not* part of the conditions I agreed to!"

"It was not. Believe it or not, the Dur cat trial is to increase your likelihood of survival."

"Why can't I go Above without it?"

"We *have* to be sure you're ready. This is not a breaking of our contract, merely a condition for carrying it out. Like learning what the Runners had to teach was. You didn't object to that." The godi glanced at his sister. "Frigdis tells me you no longer need the table to See. That means you will be able to communicate with us at our regular Seeing time if in need, just by Seeing us, then saying what you have to say. We'll 'export' you tomorrow to a Place of Leaving close to the south side of Dur Peak. That will be quick, because time, as I have said, is short and this will be safer than showing you the way through the tunnels."

Egil knew the godi was politely telling him it was safer for the Watchers if he did not yet know the tunnels, oath or no oath.

The next day, Egil stood in a small, bright room on the upper level of the Watchers' community, awaiting his "exporting." On the wall in front of him hung a picture of a Place of Leaving, much like the one to which the Runners had brought him, but in the distance behind this one rose the stark, gray slopes of Dur Peak, home range of the Dur cats. Egil wore his custom backpack, with a

selection of the snares the Runners used tied to it, and
he carried a stunner of Rigellian manufacture on his belt,
probably Aneala's. The Watchers had told him to visualize
the Place of Leaving, to feel the bite of early spring, to
smell the cold, wet wind off Dur Peak, then they had
left him. The Runner had told him that a Dur queen had
occupied a den on the west slope of the mountain, just
inside the tree line, each of the four years she had been
in the Desert.

Egil looked again at the picture. The mountain was gray
rock, with sharp edges and steep inclines. Snow covered its
top and its sides glittered with ice. It was not yet Thawtime
in the Upper World, though it was close. What trees the
mountain had were short and distorted by wind and snow.
He would have to climb that and find a wild and vicious
cat somewhere on it. Then he would have to capture and
tame the cat or lose all chance of freedom and honor.

Egil looked at his equipment. Would it be enough? Would
his knowledge be enough? One hand gripped the other for
a moment. Richard Harlan. The destroyer of his hands.
Karne's sworn enemy. He had to get him. Egil concentrated
on the picture, made it concrete in his mind, but he quailed
inside. There were so many ways to fail. Was this grim
task a sign that the god had abandoned him? Or was it the
beginning of luck again, luck such as he had not had since
the miracle of functioning hands?

The next moment a blast of cold air rocked him. He was
standing on the tile of the Place of Leaving and its shield
was down. The southern slope of Dur Peak rose, stark and
gray and cold, right in front of him. Close up, it was even
more forbidding than its picture.

Egil wriggled the pack into a more comfortable position,
checked the stunner, then slipped it back into its holder and
set off across the tile. The tree line of the west slope, the
Runner had said. That was a large area, but the Runner's
information at least made a search by a stranger to the area
possible. If he had had to search the entire mountain, especially now, when the queen would have very young kits and
be very secretive . . .

He stepped over the low wall surrounding the Place and began climbing the snow-dusted slope of the first foothill. Going directly to the tree line had seemed, in the soft warmth of the Watchers' rooms, like a good plan. As Egil trudged through snow just deep enough to hide small dips and rises in the ground and as he felt the bite of an icy wind on cheeks used to the even temperatures of the Watchers' world and of Balder, he wondered if that were still a good plan. Snow would be deeper there, and the wind sharper.

The first foothill led to a second, steeper hill and that to the foot of the mountain. Egil stopped to catch his breath, open his parka to cool off, and look at the climb. The mountain rose in slabs and piles of huge, sharp-edged blocks. In places, the slope looked like a giant's staircase, in places like an impassable cliff surmounted by another impassable cliff. He glanced at the sun. He had been traveling three to four hours already.

"No wonder the cats have made a successful last stand here," Egil muttered. "Only a Jotun could climb this." He sat at the foot of one stone block, took out his water flask, and looked around.

Dur Peak rose out of a semicircular valley in the midst of the northern mountains, mountains that stretched vast unexplored distances north, east, and west into the uninhabited and uninhabitable Frozen Zone.

It's a real puzzle, Egil thought. *A thousand years here and the Gharr know no more about this area than I do.* He shook his head.

For thousands of years his ancestors had earned fame for their explorations and settlements in new lands and new worlds. Egil had thought that kind of curiosity and adventuring was normal, until he came to Starker IV. These people did not even explore their *own* world beyond the obviously habitable areas!

Egil took another gulp of water, fished a bar of dried fruit from a pocket on the inside of his parka, and thought of the way the Gharr survived—thirty to forty meters underground, living on hydroponic fruits and vegetables and whatever grains and meat the short summer produced.

Habitable is a matter of opinion, of course, Egil conceded silently.

He bit into the fruit and looked around. To the west, beyond the third range of mountains, lay Halarek Holding. Dur Peak was visible from there, poking up above its neighbors. He hoped Karne was still all right. South, beyond only one mountain range, lay the Desert of Zinn and its Runners. East beyond the mountains and beyond Zinn lay Gildport and a couple of freecities and far, far beyond that, almost on the border of the northern Frozen Zone, lay the neutral land belonging to the World Council.

So I've run through my knowledge of Starker IV's geography and it's all on the wrong side of the planet. Richard and Breven and Harlan Holding are all west of the central meridian. Egil stood, brushed snow from his behind, and began walking slowly westward, looking for a way up the mountain.

Amid a field of giant boulders, a scree slope flowed down the mountain, around a pile of stone blocks far above Egil, and then past him, away from the mountain and into the valley. Thousands upon thousands of flat chips and small round stones covered an area fifty meters wide by an unknown length, its end hidden behind a mound of rock. Wind-ragged bluepines edged the river of rock like a thin strip of sand on a river of water. Beyond them boulders stood twice the height of a man, with great gaps between them too wide to jump. The Runner's crude map had shown Egil that Dur's west face was sheer cliffs almost to the tree line and the Runner had been right. The rock river was the only conceivable way up.

A black scavenger bird floated in circles over the barrenness higher on the slope. Small rodents squeaked and whistled from among the rocks. Egil stepped onto the scree. The small rocks slid downhill under his foot. He took another step and another. He felt as if he were sliding down the slope almost as far as he had stepped up it.

Progress upward was very slow, and after an hour or so, Egil's calves began to ache. He looked up. He still had a very long way to go. He looked to either side. Passage there looked no better than it had from the foot of the mountain. Egil looked back the way he had come. A hopper crossed the spot where he had eaten his snack. From Egil's place on the slope, the dog-sized animal looked about the size of a mouse. Egil turned again to the climb.

The incline steepened rapidly. The scavenger bird above screeched, dipped, and rose again to its slow, circling path. A rock slithered from under Egil's boot. A moment later, a whole section gave way, throwing Egil onto one knee and forcing him to catch himself with his hands. Pain shot up his arms. Egil sat abruptly, gasping, cradling his hands against his chest, and rocking back and forth with the pain. He asked the god not to let him lose consciousness and slide back to the foot of the mountain. The god listened.

When the blinding agony ceased, Egil examined his hands. There was no visible damage, other than a few small cuts, but the unexpectedly severe pain did not make for optimism about the hunt. Egil waited until he could open and close his hands without flinching, then began to climb again.

On this part of the slope he had to use his hands, even though they hurt, to help pull him up the slope. The snow quickly made his fingers sting with cold, though the rest of him was sweating with effort. Rocks cut his skin, clittered noisily down the slope, refused to provide a secure hold. Sometimes Egil felt as if he were making no progress at all.

At last, after what seemed hours, Egil reached the pile of blocks and rounded its end. The river of scree continued three or four hundred meters more, then ended in a narrow ledge at the foot of a low cliff.

Egil sat to rest and examine his hands. They were covered with cuts and scratches and dirt. He clenched them. They still worked. He stuck them into his armpits until the fingers were warm again, then uncorked the flask, took a long drink, restored the cork, and flopped onto his back to rest. The scree made a surprisingly comfortable temporary bed. For a time, he fanned himself with the open edges of his parka and watched the clouds sail by overhead. The small clouds were no longer puffy and white and separate, but flat and gray and beginning to cling together. There was a storm coming. He had better find shelter. He studied the clouds with Runner memories for a time, then reluctantly got to his feet and turned up the slope.

The snow at the foot of the cliff, melted by water running down the stone, had turned to ice. Little streamers of ice ran downslope from the cliff, making walking treacherous. The wind, which had been with him since the Place of Leaving, had died to light gusts of air that smelled damp.

Egil looked up the cliff. Bare brown tendrils of some sort of vine hung over the edge and Egil could see a few tips of bluepine branches. The cliff face was grooved and nearly vertical, with no visible chinks for hand- and foot-holds. The wind rose and a small hard pellet of snow stung Egil's cheek. He looked around. The shelter here was either among the huge blocks of stone, where all he would be sheltered from was the wind, or among the bluepines at the edges of the scree river, but the pines were thin and so distorted by the wind that they would provide precious little protection. He looked at the sky again. Perhaps he had an hour before the storm broke, perhaps less. He looked at the cliff. Here he could not climb it, not with his hands weak and recently hurt.

Egil picked his way carefully westward along the base of the cliff. He reached its end, which butted against an impassable rock wall. He looked again at the sky. The gray clouds hung lower and seemed to be fraying at the bottom. It was going to snow for a while. Perhaps he could shelter himself in the corner between the two rock faces, pitch his small tent on the scree, or stretch his ground cloth between poles and wrap himself in his nightbag. Then he thought of the immense piles of snow he had seen at the feet of cliffs, snow that had fallen over the edge after storms or had collected there when the wind hit the rock wall and dropped its load of snow. He could suffocate there.

That brought memories of the past spring's snow, and the long flight through it, and wandering into the whiteness, and falling, and—Egil brought his thoughts up with a jerk. There had to be some way to stay warm . . .

He walked slowly back along the cliff. Midway he found a cleft that ran to the top. It must have been hidden from the other direction by the shadow of its jutting eastern edge. At the bottom, the cleft was entirely doable, but in the dimming light, he could not be sure what the distances and surfaces at the top were like. The cleft did not seem to widen much. He would have to take the chance that it did not. At worst, he would only have wasted the time going up and coming back down. Egil shed his pack, took a long, thin rope from it, and tied one end of the rope to the pack. The other end he wound around his waist. Egil slid into the cleft, set his back against one side and his feet against the other, and began to scoot upward.

Egil reached the top exhausted and covered with wind-blown ice, but whole. It was almost dark, and ice pellets clicked against the stone of the cleft and whispered against the pines. He stretched out across the pine-needle-strewn edge, leaned over, and pulled up the pack, working slowly and carefully to protect his hands. He checked the pack over quickly for holes or tears, then hoisted it over one shoulder and headed for the shelter of a pine grove several meters from the cleft. At the edge of the grove, Egil brushed as much ice and snow from himself as he could, crawled under branches already bent to the ground with icy new snow, and brushed snow from himself again. He looked around, selected a thick trunk with only a dusting of snow around it, crawled over to it, and sat down.

For many minutes Egil was content just to breathe without needing to move. The air around him was cold, but still. All around him ice-coated branches rattled in the wind. Sometimes the movement loosened great lumps of snow, which fell from the branches with soft thuds. Egil prayed the branches did not lose enough snow to expose him to the wind again. Eventually Egil lifted the pack's top flap and pulled out a tin of stew, a hard biscuit, and a second flask. He pulled the tab on the stew and, while waiting for it to heat, took a long swig from the flask. He choked a moment on the fiery liquid, then took another swig.

Ah, mead. After a year drinking the Gharr's thin wine and weak beer, he had mead again. A small compensation for being a prisoner of the Watchers. Too bad he had to tramp around in the cold and snow after a vicious cat to get any.

On the other hand, mead had to be rather hard to make here, considering living and food production conditions. Perhaps it *was* much rarer and more expensive among the Watchers than it was at home. Perhaps it *was* a special reward. Perhaps he should feel more grateful.

Egil took another drink, wiped his mouth with the back of his hand, wiped the rim of the flask with his palm, and restoppered the mead.

He *was* grateful.

He ate the warm stew and the cold biscuit, untied the nightbag from its place below the pack, crawled into the bag and pressed its edge closed until only his face was exposed, then went to sleep.

Morning light came through branches and snow as a diffuse brightness. Egil stretched, which he found difficult to do in the fastened bag, yawned, rolled over. He was thinking slow, warm thoughts of going back to sleep when an eerie yowl raised the hair on the back of his neck. He listened intently. The world around him was silent, silent as only a land covered with new snow can be. Egil scrunched lower in the bag and closed his eyes.

"Probably a Runner," he murmured as he drifted nearer and nearer sleep. "Runners have a weird howl, they say."

Again, whatever it was yowled. Again, Egil's hair stood up. Egil yanked open the fastening, sat up, pulled on gloves and cap from the pack, and crawled to the edge of the trees to look cautiously out. There were ritual greetings with the Runners, greetings he needed to remember exactly if he expected aid or information: The Runners did not kill other humans except when threatened first, or so they had told him, but the lack of a proper greeting ritual was considered a threat. He saw no one on the white mountainside.

Egil examined the mountain carefully. It sloped somewhat more gently here than it did below the cliff and was dotted with pines and clumps of what Egil knew as pricklybush, a shrubby, sharp-needled evergreen. Snow lay knee-deep or better everywhere and sparkled in the morning sun, but there was no sign of humans or human passage. Egil examined the slope again. Below him, where he thought the yowl had come from, a large black cat dragged the limp, twitching body of a hopper from under some pines onto the open snow. The cat stood sharply black against the white, perhaps a hundred meters away, its coat gleaming in the sun, and yowled a third time.

Egil crawled silently a little farther out of the trees, ignoring the bite in the wind and the snow that fell off the branches and down the back of his neck. The cat did not seem to notice him.

I must be downwind! was his first thought. The second was, *Thanks be to Thor and Heimdal for that, if half what the Gharr say about the Dur cats is true.*

Two very small black cats came tumbling from behind a clump of pricklybush and fell upon the hopper. The queen backed away and lay down to watch.

So close! How could he catch her?

The queen spread her paw and began licking long, long claws that glittered in the sun as she cleaned them. Her every movement, even in bathing, told of strength out of proportion to her size. Egil thought of the killing rage and what he would look like afterward if the cat went into one.

Shreds, he told himself. *Small shreds. That's what I'd be. These cats only kill. Even their food: I'd wager they don't even play with their food first, like other cats.*

The kits staggered a little way from the kill and lay down together in a lump. The cat rose and stalked over to clean up whatever bits the kits had left. Heavy muscles slid and flexed under the sleek black coat. She crouched and chewed and glanced now and then toward the sleeping kits. The longer Egil watched, the more certain he was that if catching the queen alive were possible—and he was sure it was not—taming her would be impossible; and if he wanted Harlan, if he wanted ever to be free again, he had to produce a tamed cat. He would have to take a kit and, considering how vigilant the queen was, that, too, would be very tricky.

Egil lay flat, dropped his chin onto his crossed arms, and waited. Eventually she would finish and go. Perhaps he could follow her and get at least a clue to where the den was. Perhaps in the meantime, something would give him an idea of how to snatch a cub.

The queen checked to be sure she had missed no scrap, then roused the kittens and stalked off up the mountain. The kittens tumbled and bounced and wrestled in her wake, sometimes forgetting they were supposed to be following, so the queen had to come back for them and remind them with a clawed tap on the shoulder or rear end.

She'll hunt for herself later, probably, unless the tom does the hunting for her, Egil told himself. That was a chilling thought: two adult Dur cats at the den. Egil swallowed hard. *Surely not. Such aid is rare in cats. The tom was more likely to view the kits as easy meat.*

For four days Egil followed the cats' trail, losing it on bare rock or on flats where the wind had blown the tracks away, or where the cats could walk on top of the snow crust and Egil broke through. Each time he found the queen again by her yowl calling the kits to supper. At dusk every day he worked on a pine-bark sack to line the nightbag and, he hoped, hold a violent and frightened Dur kitten for several hours. He fastened the sheets of pine bark together with a crude thread made from pine roots. Each evening Egil also worked on the cage he would need, even for a kitten. He made it of green-wood pine branches, insetting them with his knife and reinforcing every joint with pine-root ties. He wished for pitch to glue the pine to the joints, but good pitch required long cooking and special recipes that only master shipwrights knew.

On the fifth day, when the queen called the kits to supper, she was standing only a few meters away from the den. Egil, carefully downwind, watched the kits ripping the largish creature she had brought them, which was by that time torn to unrecognizable small pieces.

There's no tom, he told himself. *She wouldn't do this if the tom were a danger. I haven't seen even one cat print that doesn't belong to one of these three.*

Egil crouched behind a pricklybush and watched the meal. He watched the queen shoo the kits into the den. He watched her stalk over to the kill to begin her own meal. She ripped all the meat from a long, straight bone, then rolled a skull into her reach and began carefully licking out its contents.

Even accustomed as he had become to the brutalities of war in his year on Starker IV, the realization of what the queen was eating was too much for Egil's stomach. He dropped his face into the snow and hoped the cold would stifle his violent urge to vomit or could at least muffle the noise.

I was thinking this would be so easy! All I'd have to do was wait until she was off hunting for herself and far enough away she wouldn't hear any squealing. So easy! So stupid! This cat's killed a Runner for her children's supper!

CHAPTER 7

When Egil at last raised his head, the queen was gone and the kits were asleep. Egil carefully lifted and aimed his stunner, keeping his movements as silent as possible. He hoped his carefully estimated setting was not too high for the little animals. He fired. Both kits went so limp they looked dead.

"Heimdal, no!" All the time and effort and the pain of the climb. Wasted. Freedom lost forever.

Egil sprinted toward the kits, capture sack and stunner in hand. Artificial respiration. A shaking. What would help? His fingers brushed the small first-aid box on his belt. A stimulant—

Heimdal, let them not be dead!

The queen yowled very close by. Egil spun toward the sound. The queen hit him in the left shoulder, making him stagger, lose the catch bag, and fall. Egil went cold with fear. The queen's claws sank half through his arm. Egil jammed his right forearm against her throat to hold her away. Her teeth clicked shut only centimeters from the side of his neck. Egil strained to turn the stunner into the cat's side, but turning his wrist against the cat's pressure on his forearm was very difficult. Her rear claws ripped his legs. Pain burned from thigh to knee. Egil fired the stunner. The cat only flinched.

Egil knew a moment of blank horror, then the cat's teeth

tore through the thick layers of his parka and scarf and high-necked sweater, grazing his skin. Egil shoved desperately with his arm and fired the stunner again. The stunner didn't even slow her down! Fear brought hot, burning bile into Egil's throat. He was lost. He was going to die sliced ingloriously, cut to ribbons by a wild animal in a wilderness on a backwater planet and no one would ever know. Even in this last thing, he could not perform as an Olafsson ought!

The cat's teeth closed high on his shoulder. Bright needles of pain set his shoulder on fire. In desperation, Egil lifted the stunner to club the cat with it. The power light showed green. Green. It was still set low to knock out kittens. The cat dug in with her front claws, then her hind claws ripped higher. Egil felt muscle tear and hot blood stream down his leg. Teeth clenched against a scream, Egil thumbed the stunner's control knob to maximum and fired.

The cat went limp and let go of him. Egil felt her neck with the side of his stunner hand. No pulse. Egil took a deep unsteady breath. He felt as if he had been fighting the cat for hours. His whole body was shaking. The Dur cats' rage apparently killed a lot faster to observers than to victims. He looked at his hands. They bled from cuts made by the ice crust on the ground, but were otherwise whole. He clenched and unclenched them. They still worked. The god had restored his luck.

Egil tried to sit up. Everything went dark for a moment. When the whirling blackness went away, Egil looked down at himself. He sat in bloody snow, snow stirred and gouged and mounded by the struggle. The cat had ripped his left leg open in long, deep stripes from hip to below the knee. His right leg was not so badly torn, but it, too, was red and steaming with blood. His shoulder bled slowly from innumerable puncture wounds. Punctures never bled a lot, but they quickly became infected and cat bites were notoriously dirty. He was in deep trouble.

Egil glanced toward the kittens. They were beginning to stir. If they awoke completely, they, too, would be dangerous. He lifted the stunner. The power had almost run out. One or two shots more at maximum and the stunner would be dead. He must do something about the kittens before he no longer could. Already he felt faint from blood loss, and he had nothing but snow and the small pads in the med-kit to press against the wounds to make the bleeding stop. There were too many wounds. His thoughts swirled in the hazy twilight between consciousness and unconsciousness. If he fainted, the kittens would rouse and run away—if they did not try to eat him first. If they ran away, he would have to do everything again. If they tried to eat him . . . He could not rouse more than an academic interest in the speculation.

Egil swayed and just barely kept himself from falling over. Cold bit into unprotected skin. It was spring here. It didn't feel like it. Harlan would escape in the spring. He had to escape in the spring. Spring had flowers and warm sunshine, even on Starker IV. The caravan roads were dry and the winds at flying altitudes died down. Harlan could be back in control by the summer fighting season. Summer meant fliers and troop transports and dry ground. And the Gharr always left their absolutely secure underground Holdings to fight each other on the surface.

Egil shook his head. Impossible to understand. Gas would be a good weapon here. But it had only been used once. The lord of House Kerinnen had shoved gas canisters into the ventilation systems of his enemies during The War. That gas caused the mutation that caused the Sickness. Even now, 140 years later, the Sickness killed most females of the Families. The Families had destroyed House Kerinnen completely. Not a stone, not a passageway, not a drop of Kerinnen blood survived. Egil looked down at himself. Not a drop of Egil Olafsson's blood was going to survive, either. Egil watched it drip onto the snow. He was bleeding to death.

A weak mewling from the kittens roused Egil enough to think about them. He had to have a kitten or he could not help Karne; he could not take revenge on Harlan. Harlan. He must kill Harlan. He had to have a Dur cat first. But there were no cats here, only kittens.

Egil made his eyes focus on the small black bodies by the den. Catch a kitten. He had to put a kitten in the bag before they woke completely. His injuries. There must be *something* he could do about them.

One thing at a time, he told himself, then another. One thing. First, kitten.

Egil crawled to the catch bag, which was lying where the queen had first attacked him, then crawled toward the kittens. Each movement increased the burning pain in his legs. Each meter seemed like ten. Egil felt as if he were looking down a tunnel and the kittens were a black blur in the small circle of light at tunnel's end. He paused frequently to put his head down and wait for a black wave of faintness to pass.

His fingers brushed warm, sleek fur. Egil forced his eyes to focus. The kittens. They were squirming and moaning, almost awake. Egil held the bag open with one hand and wrapped his other hand around a kitten. The weight was almost too much. His hand resisted lifting, his grip loosened against his will. He tightened his hold as best he could and slid the now-wiggling kit into the bag. He let the opening close, held it closed between his forearm and the ground, and waited, head hanging, until he regained his strength. He dragged the other kitten toward him and slid it, too, into the bag, drew the opening rope tight, and sank, belly-down, onto the snow. He rested his head on his arms. There was still the long trip downslope and he knew he could not do it. There was no possible way for him to travel any distance at all. Perhaps he could not even drag himself and his catch into the shelter of the pines again.

Egil realized later he must have passed out, for when he looked up again, the sun was on its downward journey. Cold was seeping through his sturdy outerwear. The slightest movement brought waves of faintness. The catch bag was twitching and snarling. Egil turned it over and discovered a hole being gnawed in it.

"Smart little beasts," he muttered.

He rolled over so his good shoulder pressed the hole flat. The kits snarled and spit. Egil knew he had run out of time. He had to call for help. If his luck still held, he could force an image into the evening Seeing.

He formed a picture of the mountain slope and of the Dur cat lying sprawled in blood. He thought hard of Frigdis and held the image of the cat sprawled in blood until his eyes and mind could no longer endure the concentration. Nothing came back. He had not reached them. He was finished.

Egil drew a deep, shuddering sigh. This was not how the Viking kind were supposed to die, alone on a cold mountain, bleeding to death from lack of the wit to remember how fiercely a queen defends her young. He should have died in battle defending the guardpost, or full of the honors or accomplishments of a lifetime in diplomacy or science or trade. He owed it to his family to have *done* something with his life. And his family would never know what happened to him unless Solveig or Mother did a Seeing. But the gods would know. Even on this frigid, gods-forsaken world, the gods would know. Perhaps they would let him into Valhal, anyway. Probably not. Why would the gods, doomed themselves, feel any mercy for a young man doomed always to stand out of fame's path?

"I have not even the strength for a death song," he whispered to the open sky.

A black scavenger circled overhead. The kittens writhed and snarled in the bag. Egil felt the life seeping from him onto the snow. Everything went dark.

Egil roused slightly. He heard voices, a shout, the *shush-shush* of skis, but could not bring himself to open his eyes and pay more attention. He was lifted a little and set down again. The swishing of skis through snow was almost by his ear now. What did the great god Njord have to do with the dead?

Now and again Egil was aware of voice and other sounds, sometimes of an abrupt movement, and once he felt as if he were hanging in space. Perhaps the Valkyries came for even such as he. Nothing mattered anymore. Karne's enemy would overwhelm him and he, Egil, could no longer do his part to prevent that.

"I'm sorry, Karne," he whispered.

"Egil? Egil, come you back!"

It was Frigdis's voice, and the sharpness of anxiety in it demanded Egil's attention. He did not want to pay attention. The dark place where he lay was so quiet and peaceful.

"Egil? Don't slip away again. Look at me!"

Reluctantly, Egil opened his eyes. Frigdis stood beside his sleeping bench, her face taut and white. He was in the infirmary again. As he watched, the strain disappeared and Frigdis smiled.

"Ei, I thought you would never come back from where you've been roaming."

A snarling sound came from the floor near her feet. Frigdis looked down, then looked at Egil. "The surviving kitten hungers. You will feed it today. There is no other way to win its heart." She looked down again. "Perhaps there is *no* way. She killed her sister and we don't know why." She looked at Egil again. "Some among us doubt you would be able to capture Harlan without killing him. Or if you'll be able to catch him at all, considering an animal outthought you so."

Egil propped himself up on one elbow and looked down at his bandaged legs. The movement made his bitten shoulder ache. It *had* been very stupid to try for the kittens without either killing the queen or making sure she was out of hearing. Well, he would pay for that stupidity for some time. Perhaps for the rest of his life if the opinions Frigdis cited were majority opinions. By Heimdal! They could not be majority opinions! Egil collapsed back onto the bench with a groan.

Frigdis patted Egil's unbandaged shoulder. "Rest easy. We have persuaded the others, at least for now, that they underestimated the instincts of a Dur cat. The Harlan does not operate on instinct and that is to your advantage. Perhaps." She smiled again. "You have only lost a few days this time. And your cat is here on the floor, where it always has your scent nearby." She laughed. "It required an awfully strong cage for an animal so small. You can begin taming it as soon as you feel mobile enough."

Frigdis patted his unbandaged shoulder again and left.

Egil watched the doorway through which Frigdis had gone long after she was out of sight. He was lucky to have such a friend among the Watchers. And he *had* survived his fight with the Dur cat. He *had* brought back a Dur cat. All three good luck. Perhaps the god would stay with him now.

Luck did stay with Egil. He recovered quickly, though his legs were somewhat stiff for a month. The taming of the kitten progressed, though more slowly than Egil liked. Most important, Richard Harlan had not yet broken out of his prison. All would have been for nothing if Harlan had escaped before Egil succeeded in taming the cat.

Egil began the taming by feeding the kitten by hand. If she did not accept food from him, she did not eat. She had not eaten the entire time he was unconscious. She did not eat afterward until she was too weak to stand. Egil felt both anger and admiration for the little creature. She did not like captivity any better than he and she was doing the only thing she could to be free. When the little animal was finally too weak to resist him, Egil took her from her cage into his lap and clipped her claws. The kitten glared at him with baleful almond eyes.

"Defiant to the end, little one?" He risked a quick soothing stroke down her back. "I won't let you starve yourself to death. Sorry."

He pried open the little cat's jaws, took from his own mouth raw meat he had pre-chewed, and laid the meat on her tongue. She only glared at him. Egil opened her jaws again, poked the meat to the back of her mouth, held her head back, and stroked her throat until she had to swallow. She refused to swallow the next bite herself, and the next, and the next.

For two days Egil force-fed the kitten; for another week he chewed the food for her. It was the third week before she would take food from his hand. At first, she took the food, then tried to slash Egil's hand. Then she took the food and ignored Egil. Then she took the food eagerly and purred afterward. At this stage, Egil let her out of her cage and let her roam the tiny cubicle that was his quarters. He began to introduce her to the Watchers, one at a time, and confined her to her cage each time she growled or took a swipe at any of them.

Egil made her a studded red leather collar of the sort that the cats had once worn in the gladiatorial ring to protect their throats. He knew the collar would not protect her from human weapons, but it made her look owned and red was a very striking color on her. With the help of tapes from the library about the ancient art of lion-taming, Egil began training the cat, which he named Skadi, to be his battle companion: to come when called, to attack on command, to stop an attack. This last was the hardest and, though Egil practiced with her a lot in the Upper World, she would not learn it. Egil gave up this part of her training, hoping it would take on her when she was older. This decision meant he would have to leave her behind on his hunt for Harlan. She would be too great a danger.

Egil did not want to leave her behind. He had hoped she could catch meat for them both so he would not have to set snares for fresh rations, but she was still too unskilled to be reliably successful. He had also wanted her company. She had begun to feel like a friend, and here among the Watchers he had no other friends but Frigdis.

Egil had just finished a day on the surface training Skadi and was stripping for a bath when a young boy came bursting into his room. The tired cat growled and took a swipe at him, leaving shallow pink scratches on his leg. Egil cuffed her, then tied her to a ring in the wall near her cage as punishment, because she had already outgrown the cage. The boy glanced at the scratches, then blurted his message. "You must come at once. Richard Harlan has escaped!"

Egil threw on a long, everyday sark and followed the boy to the great hall, where the godi was waiting in his high seat. Frigdis, Magnus, Arne, Floki, and the other members of the godi's housecarls were sitting on the long bench across the table from him. Egil halted in front of the godi, made a perfunctory bow, and sat in one of the two or three vacant places along the bench.

"Floki, summarize what you Saw," the godi ordered.

Floki rose. "I was on my shift, surveying the Upper

World. I was concentrating my attention on Breven and Harlan and Halarek, as is usual lately."

"There was unusual clamor at Breven," Arne broke in. "So Floki went back in time and came forward to the point of disturbance. Richard Harlan, wearing a deacon's gray robe and hood, slipped out the door to the garden undetected. He murdered the guard who tried to stop him from leaving the compound. The clamor was a result of discovering the guard's corpse."

Floki looked at Egil. "No deacon leaves the compound unless sent by the abbot or for a family emergency. It was several hours, at nightmeal, before the community discovered Harlan's absence," he continued. He stopped to rub the back of his neck. "Sorry. It was a long Seeing. By the time the escape was discovered, Harlan was in the foothills north of Breven."

"He dare not trust his own men," Arne added. "His cousins may be fighting each other and the vassals for control of the House, but they are all united in determining that Harlan shall not return. Not alive, at least."

Egil felt a surge of disappointment. He would have much company on the hunt. Perhaps too much company. He swung a leg painfully back over the bench to leave. He tried to keep the disappointment out of his voice. "Then you have no need of me."

The godi held up a hand and motioned him to turn back to the table. "On the contrary. As we told you before, we want Harlan *alive*. The cousins most definitely do not." The godi studied Egil as if he could read minds. "As soon as you can pack your equipment, you must go. Remember, you must not only capture Harlan but keep him alive. The cousins will just make the job a little harder."

Egil had heard stories about clan assassins. "A little harder" was probably the understatement of the decade.

The godi pushed a small round object across the table to Egil. "This is a trap controller. There are ruins all over the north of Starker IV and this will be a long chase. You may need this. Harlan isn't running toward his own Holding, but toward Kingsland, his old trustee, and he's running through the Frozen Zone, because the Gharr never go there. We cannot reach you this time to help; you will be beyond all Places of Leaving. You will be entirely alone against him. Are you ready?"

"I'm ready, gentlehom."

CHAPTER 8

While Egil collected his supplies and equipment and called Skadi from her wanderings to confine her to his room, the godi assembled a last-minute Seeing. In a very rare departure from tradition, the godi included the Runner who had taught Egil in the group. What the group Saw was Harlan hiking north toward a horizon that steamed or smoked.

"That makes your search easier, off-worlder," said the Runner. "There are only two areas like that in the Frozen Zone. One is directly north of Loch and full of volcanoes. The other is full of boiling water and geysers and bubbling mud and lies north along lines through Konnor Holding and Council ground."

Egil had shaken his head. "That's nowhere near Harlan Holding. He's going the wrong direction!"

Frigdis snorted. "Council and the minor Houses in the area had troops covering the ground around Harlan and Odonnel within hours of Harlan's escape. He can't go home." Frigdis's tone suggested it had been about time for that kind of action.

The godi looked Egil in the eye. "He did not escape Breven without help, of course. Someone left a cache of supplies and cold-weather clothes not a kilometer from the compound. Whether that helper meant Harlan well or ill we would have to See and there's no point. We know Harlan survived."

"But the future changes." Egil was thinking of the changes

he meant to make in Harlan's future.

The godi shrugged. "The future changes. We do the best we can."

A short time later, Egil stood on the tiles of a Place of Leaving in an icy wind, looking at the mountains he had to cross or pass between. This Place was in a bowl-like hanging valley just inside the Frozen Zone. North, east, and west of Egil lay sharp, gray mountains; south, beyond a steep drop, lay the pale green of the open steppes, newly free of snow, and the even more distant sparkle of Lake St. Paul. Egil could see a small dark blotch at the northwest end of the lake that was the free city of Loch. The Retreat House of Breven lay at the lake's other end, hidden by the pine forest that surrounded it.

How easy it must have been for Harlan to escape, once he was beyond the compound, Egil thought. *There's been no snow for a couple weeks now, and what's left on the ground down there is mostly ice, yet the ground still freezes hard at night. He'd leave no tracks to follow.*

What kind of help had Harlan had or would he have—besides the cache—and how much? Egil wondered. Why was he running north, where no one and nothing lived? And why on foot? Egil had himself been bundled out of the Watchers' community much too fast to give Harlan's behavior much thought until now. Fliers would be quick transport to Kingsland, but they were also very visible on land or in the air, easy to attack, and would show up in the Gild's Orbital pix, even if they landed in the Frozen Zone. Especially if they landed in the Frozen Zone. The Gild would be sure to report anything as unusual as that without considering itself "interfering" in native affairs. Just last Uhl, the Gild had used Orbital pix to help locate a crashed flitter full of children, the result of one of Karne's vassal's stubbornness in refusing to give Karne legal homage. When that vassal was finally forced to yield and to give hostages, it was too late in Uhl to fly safely.

It was Uhl before last, though, Egil told himself. *I wasn't awake for last Uhl.*

He was awake now, and alive, and it was spring, his favorite time of year. The late-morning air felt soft against his cheeks and smelled of aspen buds and running water and wet earth and leaves. For a moment Egil savored being in the Upper World. He was free! There was air, real air, after months and months of breathing recirculated stuff. Egil could not stop himself from taking big breaths and enjoying spring's warmth and smells and dampness. He stretched high and gave a wordless shout of joy at being free at last. An echo beat back at him from the gray rock walls. Egil stood very still and listened until the last faint echo died to silence. Now he heard everywhere around him water trickling quietly, sneaking silently out from under banks of snow in drips and streamlets, running through the cracks and grooves in the tiles. Softened snow fell with faint, crackly plops from snowdrift to ground. A wik-wik perched on a bare branch and called, "Who's there? Who's there?"

Egil took one more extravagant breath of air, then bent to check his equipment. Nightbag, fighting ax, stunner, shovel, two-pot, thermo, med-kit, backpack and all its contents, tunnel-trap controller—all were there. He was as ready as he was going to be and Richard was just around the corner, in a manner of speaking. Egil hefted the pack. It seemed heavier than he remembered. He shoved his arms through the pack straps, checked the equipment hanging from straps on the outside to be sure it was all secure, then struck out northeastward along an old caravan road that ran from the swamps of Londor to the edge of the Druma Holding. A chase through the Frozen Zone looked to be a long, cold trip, though it would soon be summer here along the Zone's edge, and Egil saw no reason to tramp through the colder foothills when he could follow a warm, springtime road. Only when he saw the landmarks from yesterday's Seeing would he go into the hills.

The going on the hard-packed earth was easy and probably safe. There were no trees beside the road for any sort of attacker to hide behind, just knee-high silvery-tan grass, flattened by the winter's snow. If someone had stayed behind to keep pursuit off Harlan's tail, he could not conceal himself here. If Harlan had taken the road and then left it, the silvery grass would show it.

Egil stayed with the road about three hours, until it crossed a narrow river valley over an old stone bridge. The gravel bank on the far side of the bridge had been stirred by several pairs of feet, all of them heading north. Egil studied the few good prints he found. Men in military boots, marching north. Harlan's escort? Or his cousins' assassins? Or would the cousins themselves come hunting him? Egil thought the last unlikely, from what he knew of Gharr politics: Any cousin left behind would claim head-of-House, perhaps murdering the heirs of any who went hunting. Egil sat at the end of the bridge and relaxed himself for a Seeing. What came was a view of Richard himself, sitting alone in a long narrow valley beside a thermo, warming hands that were blue with cold and shaking with the force of his shivering. Beyond him, visible above the hills, dark streamers of smoke drifted eastward across the sky. Whether Harlan was waiting for an escort or on his way to meet one, or planning his return to power, or setting up a coup against Council, or just wishing he were warm, Egil had no way of knowing. He did know he was Seeing Harlan's future. He knew Harlan was waiting to get warm. He hoped he failed.

Egil turned and followed the swath of disturbed gravel into the foothills. An icy wind blew down the narrow valley, making Egil tighten his collar around his neck. Trees gathered on the lower slopes, aspen and blue pine and heaven's wood and flame trees. Shadows lengthened, making the trees' leafless branches into long, spidery things that swayed across the grass in the rising wind. A few flakes of snow flew on that wind, too, but they were the thin, see-through kind that last only long enough to leave a tiny cold mark on parka or cheek or eyelid.

Egil looked at the dropping sun. There was not much light left. It would be best to find a stopping place for the night and continue his hunt in the morning. Egil planned to be warm and for that he must find shelter from possible observers so he could build his night fire and set up the two-man tent without fear of surprise attack. He wished he knew if this was the valley he had Seen Harlan in. Unfortunately, the Seeing could not pinpoint places, especially not places no one in the Seeing had ever visited. To be discovered by Harlan would be fatal, because Harlan would not risk leaving anyone alive who knew his location.

Two days later, Egil got his first warning that he was closing on Harlan. He smelled burned meat. He stopped at first smelling, listened, looked around thoroughly, and then went on. A few hundred meters farther he found the body of a very young man dressed in winter camouflage, one side burned to a crisp by a beamer. He had probably been an assassin. He was certainly very, very dead.

Egil looked down at the body for the space of a long breath. "You forgot the lord of Harlan is a marksman and duelist, didn't you?" he said softly. "Well, you won't make that sort of mistake again. You won't make *any* mistake again."

Egil crouched beside the young man and carefully searched his pockets. He had either carried no identification or Harlan had taken whatever he had had. Assassins never carried identification. The dead man's beamer had charge enough left for only one or two full-power shots, not enough to make carrying it worthwhile for Harlan, apparently. Egil made sure its safety was on, then stuck it into his belt. Beamers were very nasty weapons, but they occasionally had uses.

Egil moved much more carefully after that. Perhaps half an hour farther along lay a small lake and beside the lake was a small camp. Harlan had set up a two-man tent on the lake's north shore, at the foot of a south-facing mountain. The mountain acted as a giant solar reflector and kept the lake, and its valley, tolerably warm. Especially for Starker IV in the late spring, Egil amended to himself. Nonetheless, Harlan had a fire going and was warming his hands over it and shivering. He appeared to be alone. Egil's hand crept to his stunner. It would be a chancy shot at this distance, but he might never again have such a good opportunity. He drew the stunner and sighted along its barrel. He imagined Harlan wilting onto the gravel streambed, never to rise again. Never to kill again. Karne protected. Vengeance attained.

But a shot from hiding won't satisfy the requirements of a proper act of vengeance. I'll stand up and challenge him.

Egil's muscles tensed to stand, then his Academy training stopped him. *Don't let your own culture distort clear thinking.* That had been drummed into all the cadets again and again, yet Egil had been about to act by Balder's rules and would have ended up dead. Richard Harlan would have beamed him the moment he stood up.

The hot flush of shock and fear made Egil feel boneless for a moment. No fame. No vengeance. No honor. Just dead. From overeagerness and pride. Dead. What was almost as bad, now he thought of it, was that Harlan had had secret help from someone, some House, and that secret help endangered Karne almost as much as Harlan himself, because it opened vast possibilities for treachery. Was it just Kingsland? The Watchers said Harlan fled toward Kingsland, but Kingsland could be a front for someone else. Or not. In either case, Karne did not know any of what was happening and his ignorance put him at great risk.

Egil looked away from Harlan and temptation. Vengeance would be sweet. It would feel good for a time, but the godi had said nine years in Breven was, to Harlan, far worse than anything Egil could do to him. The godi had also said Harlan's continued existence was necessary to this world and godis were usually right.

Egil considered what he knew more carefully. Harlan had had help at Breven but had run into the wilderness alone. That said he did not trust men of his own House to guard him. The fact that he was sitting beside a lake might say something, too. Perhaps the other footprints had belonged to an advance force of some sort, men who went ahead to be sure the Heir in Harlan ran into no danger. On the other hand, perhaps they belonged to assassins.

Harlan stood and began folding his tent. Once it was down, Egil could see strips of meat hanging from a small rack smoking over a tiny fire. Egil nodded, understanding

Harlan's lingering here. He had been hunting. Since he had been hunting, then he had clearly decided he could not afford to be pinpointed by having food air-dropped to him. Or maybe his ally was not willing to chance being seen and identified. Or both. Egil wondered if Council would execute Harlan if it captured him. He wondered if Harlan were wondering, too, because he was most definitely taking a path far beyond any chance of accidentally encountering other human beings.

In a sudden flash of understanding, Egil saw what difficulties his original intention to kill Harlan would have made for Karne. What was happening in House Harlan could be very important to House Halarek, *had* to be very important to Halarek. Harlan had a plan. He had at least one ally willing to help him escape Council. He had wealth and political power beyond Karne's dreams. He was running through the Zone for his own good reasons. To disguise his destination? To protect himself from his cousins? Certainly to hide from Council patrols and fliers. Perhaps Harlan also knew something about the Frozen Zone that no other Gharr did.

Egil stared down at the man stuffing cooking utensils into a pack. There would be a lot of satisfaction in just pounding the stuffing out of the duke-designate. But personal vengeance no longer seemed such a good idea, not after what the godi had said, not after what Egil himself had just figured out. Killing Harlan would end all possibility of learning either his intentions or his ally. Egil felt a powerful surge of disappointment. His plans for vengeance, his oath of vengeance, must be set aside in Karne's best interest. How he could escape the taint of oath-breaker he did not know. On this world it would not matter. Most of the lords of the Nine had no sense of honor, anyway. But at home . . .

Harlan was shouldering his pack, sliding a stunner into its belt case, and climbing out of the valley. Egil noted the second weapon. He followed as quickly as was safe. Harlan hiked up a broad incline that led to a low, wide pass between two steep mountains. Once he was through the pass, Egil saw tall columns of smoke or steam drifting upward on the northern horizon, just like in the Seeing. Harlan followed a long, narrow valley with a frozen river down its middle. Egil recognized the valley of his Seeing.

The next day and the next, Harlan marched north toward the columns of smoke or steam. Each night, Harlan sat beside a fire and warmed his hands, just like in the Seeing.

His clothes aren't as good as mine, Egil thought the first night. *I'm thinner-blooded by far and I'm warm.*

Snow fell almost every night and the ground was always frozen. Occasionally a warm wind blew down the valley, but it was not a spring wind. It smelled of sulphur and smoke. Anywhere out of this wind, the air was bitter cold. Even in the warmest parts of the day, the brooks and puddles were ice clear through. Egil had to keep reminding himself it was late spring farther south. The glow just over the horizon grew brighter and brighter and Egil felt more and more uneasy about Harlan's destination.

Harlan climbed a ridge thinly covered with trees and pricklybush plants. He walked to the edge of the ridge and stood to look at what was beyond it. Egil slipped from skimpy tree to skimpy tree so he could see, too. The ridge dropped off as cliff on its far side and an immense plain stretched out of sight from the cliff's base, its edges concealed by clouds or smoke. The cliff wound sinuously in both directions along the edge of the plain as if, in some very ancient time, the basin had dropped two or three hundred meters. Heat rose along the face of the cliff and the smell of sulphur was overwhelming.

Near the base, dark crevices and holes steamed ominously. A section of the valley floor heaved, showing glowing red to pink areas that turned charcoal-colored as they cooled. Other areas steamed, or showed red or pink through narrow cracks and lines. Here and there, the abrupt cones of volcanoes stood like grim black monuments. Some of these smoked and some looked long cold and dead. Egil felt a strong stirring of apprehension. He did not want to travel through such an area. Even less did he want to track Harlan through an area with no cover. He would have to find his own path through the treacherous footing and all the knowledge the Runner had given him could not help here. Harlan would have a map, at least. He was too smart to risk his hide without very good odds of surviving the trip. Knowledge did not guarantee safety, though. Egil thought of his own cousin, who had known Balder's thermal areas very well and yet had died when supposedly secure ground turned out to be only a thin crust over boiling water. No, he did not want to go down there.

Harlan stood silhouetted against the burning landscape a moment too long. A beamer bolt flashed out of a clump of thick-leaved spiny plants eastward along the cliff top. The warning sizzling sound followed, but too late for Harlan, who squawked and dropped to the ground. Was he dead? Egil felt a brief flash of anger. He had given up vengeance, decided to break a sacred oath, and some *nithing* of an assassin had killed Harlan!

Don't jump to stupid conclusions, another side of him said. *Harlan's a very clever man. He may just have done what any reasonable person would do: made himself a smaller target.*

The air held the electric, burned smell of a beamer. Egil looked but saw no one in the thicket. The assassin, if he were clever, would be somewhere else now. Egil looked again at Harlan. The duke-designate was scrambling, crouched over, toward the nearest shelter, a large rock. He was cradling one hand in the other and cursing.

A lucky man, Egil thought. Or a clumsy assassin. That was more likely. Clumsiness also made the assassin most likely a member of House Harlan. Professional assassins couldn't afford mistakes. On the other hand, Harlan's father, Duke Asten Harlan, had been so inept at assassination and ambush that he had become a joke, at least in Halarek.

Another beamer bolt flashed. Harlan flinched and cursed.

Harlan was now too near for Egil's comfort, especially if the sniper were as inept as his first two shots suggested. Egil stretched out as flat as he could. He felt quite sure Harlan had not been hit the second time. The shot had just come too close for his comfort.

Gods! Egil thought. *It has to be a cousin. No self-*

respecting professional assassin would miss such an important target once, let alone twice. It's not a Runner. They don't have beamers. Egil swallowed hard. Beamers were terrible, cruel, effective weapons. He had seen Karne beamed by an incompetent (because Karne lived) assassin and he remembered Karne's weeks and weeks of pain. Karne had not used a beamer since.

Egil studied the clump of spiny plants. How many tries would the man make? This time he saw the muzzle-flash as the beamer fired. Harlan had, too. He fired his own beamer at the spot. The plants smoldered, then burned. Egil waited for the results with a soldierly detachment that surprised him. In his eyes, there was no contest. Harlan was a duelist; the assassin had already failed twice to kill. The assassin would be dead, like the one in the woods back by the lake.

Harlan waited. Egil waited. No more bolts came. Harlan waited a long time. Finally he raised himself to a crouch. When no beam came then, he stood, hesitated, then walked cautiously toward the remains of the spiny thicket, his beamer in his hand. He walked around the thicket, kicked something.

"Natan, you fool!" Harlan said in a contemptuous tone. He turned his back on the would-be killer and started down the trail again.

The competence of this "Natan" aside, I have serious competition for Harlan's skin, Egil told himself grimly. *If there were two assassins, there will probably be more. But I cannot kill him, the gods be forever damned.* Egil smiled rather grimly. The gods had always been damned and had always known it. Egil looked again at Harlan. *Assassins will make the chase more interesting, though.*

Harlan headed east along the top of the cliff, his step purposeful. Egil followed as fast as scanty cover allowed. Suddenly the sound of a flier's engine broke the winter silence. Egil wished he had paid more attention in ground training so he would at least have a good guess what kind of flier it was or how big.

The craft came over the last row of mountains. It was a big flitter, ten-passenger probably, unmarked by House colors. Harlan waved as the flitter approached, then stepped behind a clump of pricklybush to protect himself from the backwash of landing. The flitter hovered over a large open area on the cliff top. If Harlan got on, Egil's chance to learn his ally's House would vanish. If Egil stopped Harlan, he would no longer be a secret follower and Harlan would have no compunctions at all about killing Egil, from ambush or in the open.

Harlan was sprinting toward the flitter.

"That's too easy, Mister Duke-designate," Egil muttered.

He swiftly pulled the beamer from his belt, aimed down one of the engine cowls, fired, then sprinted for the cover of rocks farther away. Harlan saw the tracer. His head jerked around toward Egil's hiding place, then he dropped flat on the ground and covered the back of his head with his hands. The flitter suddenly flew apart in a ball of flame. Egil closed his eyes against the brilliance. It glowed through his eyelids for several minutes, then abruptly disappeared. Egil waited one or two minutes more. His mind told him there could be no survivors. Waiting longer to look could well mean Egil would not survive, either. That depended on whether Harlan recovered his sight before Egil did.

When Egil opened his eyes, he saw a few shards of metal, a pile of molten something, and flames here and there in the ruins. Richard of Harlan was gone.

CHAPTER 9

Egil looked around to be sure Harlan was not just in a different place, waiting for the assassin to show himself. Tracks made by a running man went east in the gravel of the cliff top. Harlan now knew someone was after him again. Egil would have to be much more careful.

Egil slid his pack off long enough to fish out a can of stew and a mug of klag. He left the beamer, its "recharge" light glowing, lying on a rock. It had no real usefulness anymore and he hated beamers, anyway. He then set out on Harlan's trail. He could think of no mistakes he had made, no opportunities he might have given Harlan to discover who was following him. Egil ripped off the tab on the klag mug, then dropped the mug and cursed. He had been wearing heavy gloves so long on this world that he had forgotten he was not wearing them here on the warm edge of the cliff. The klag spread into a steaming dark place on the ground. Egil looked at the can of stew. His stomach growled in anticipation. He looked down at the parched desert grasses at his feet. The gravel trail would be easy to follow, but the gravel would not last forever. On dry grass, Harlan's trail would be hard to follow, very hard. Could he let it grow colder while he sat somewhere and waited for stew and klag to cool enough to use? His stomach rumbled again. His tongue felt furry and dry. Egil shook his head. Later. He would have to eat a proper meal later. Harlan did not have much of a start, but he had a map and he would have no compunction about laying an ambush for his pursuer. Egil reached over his shoulder and jammed the stew back into the pack, drank long from his canteen, and munched on one of the tasteless bars of emergency rations as he walked.

Hundreds of thousands of years of human history, he grumbled, and no one has yet come up with tasty trail rations.

After several hours, Egil had followed Harlan's trail to the tree-covered crest of a wide pass. He looked over his shoulder at the steaming, smoking plain behind him. He shook his head. It had been nothing more than a landmark for Harlan, something even an idiot pilot could find. Egil examined the landscape for good spots for an ambush or traps. Nothing was obvious, but the trees would provide all kinds of cover and there was no way he could avoid the trees and still follow Harlan. Egil sprinted along the clear trail over the pass. Only a few meters down the far side, he hit a trip wire. Drinn training had him rolling as he hit the ground. A large tree crashed across the place where he had been.

Egil sat up slowly and looked long at the tree. The old bluepine had hit the ground with such force that its top had broken off. Without Drinn, he would not have rolled automatically and he would not now be alive. His shot at the flitter had changed the game. There would be traps now. Harlan planned to slow him down with traps and the suspicion of traps. Egil looked at the tree and its neighbors more closely. He himself would never have rigged a wire across such a space, but apparently Harlan knew more about such things. He would definitely have to be more careful. But more careful meant slower and that meant Harlan would increase his lead.

Egil cast back and forth the entire width of the pass until dusk, looking for some sign of Harlan. Too much of the pass was formed from sheets of lava. The bluepines had grown on one of the few places with real dirt. The only traces Egil found of Harlan's passage were a metal scratch on a rock on an icy patch beyond the trap and a discarded beamer fuel cell. The cell Egil had found by luck—a ray of sunlight had caught its porcelain case and reflected the light so it danced on a neighboring rock. There had been no burned mark to show another flitter had picked Harlan up, though he had vanished as thoroughly as if one had. The trap had delayed Egil long enough. Harlan was gone.

Egil turned and looked down the pass. Mountains stretched as far as his eye could see. Southeastward lay a broad gap between the mountains, like the seat of a giant's saddle, and the mountains on either side of this gap seemed to be lower than the rest. Perhaps, with a little imagination, Egil could see the two traces he had found of Harlan's passing pointing somewhat southeastward. He would have to check with a Seeing, but since he did not know the land well, a Seeing would not help much unless the sun appeared in it to give a direction to the image. He pitched camp before the light failed completely and then looked for a comfortable place to sit for the Seeing. He debated with himself whether a rock facing north but in the warm wind from the basin or a rock facing south that had absorbed the sun's heat would be better. He shrugged. The Seeing should not take long, so comfort was not that important.

He chose the south-facing rock and focused his inner eyes on Richard of Harlan. The first view was a past one, showing Harlan in his deacon's robes in his room at Breven. Egil rejected it and tried again. The next image was of Harlan sitting in a valley warming his hands over a thermo. The past again. Egil wished Seeing were more scientific, so he could command the right answer the first time. As things really were, not even the Watchers could command the answer they wanted from the Gift.

Egil thought of his stomach, took klag and stew and fruit from the pack, pulled the heating tabs on the klag and the stew, and settled back against the rock again. At least they'll be cool enough to eat by the time I'm done, he thought.

He tried the Seeing again, this time focusing his thoughts on the sun's direction and the mountains in front of him.

This time he Saw a broad swift river running south between widespread mountains. Harlan was crossing on a jumble of very large rocks. Egil thought he recognized Dur Peak rising stark and far to the south beyond the river. Could it really be Dur Peak? The mountain was higher than its neighbors by quite a lot, like Dur Peak, but Egil did not know what that mountain's north face looked like. Large river. Dur Peak. He looked west of the mountain in the image. There should be a gray, slab-sided neighbor, Spider Mountain. There it was. The river was the Ednov, then, and that meant Harlan was directly north of Halarek Holding. Egil remembered crossing the Ednov on the ice after the failed attack on Harlan's besiegers. *How far north is Harlan? What is he doing so close to Halarek? Is Karne under attack again now it's spring? Surely not. Trustees don't fight the clan war, do they?*

Now he had found Harlan, he could track him. Egil did as he had been trained to do: He followed Harlan backward in time. It was a very slow process, taking him hour by hour back across the river and through the mountains, something like running a film backward while skipping a lot of frames. The reel stopped on a mountain ridge visible from where Egil sat. In his mind Egil saw Harlan on the ridge, also resting and eating, and then he saw himself leaning against his rock. Egil sighed in relief. Harlan was not that far ahead of him. Egil could catch up within the day, probably, if the route to that ridge were not difficult or hard to find. Egil thought of looking ahead to the end of the chase, to see how it ended, to see where it ended and how much longer it would take, but the sybils of his family and the Watchers, too, had said that to look at one's own possible death was to ruin the rest of one's life. No one could deal well with such knowledge and, for many, such a Seeing left them waiting for death or, worse, rushing toward it. Egil expected to win the contest with the Harlan Heir, but he did not want to know if he were deluding himself.

Harlan's nearness to Halarek bothered Egil. Richard had only to cross the narrow strip of land that was Druma Holding and he was at Halarek. *What harm can one man do?*

Egil asked himself. But Harlan was no ordinary man.

Egil remembered his cooling food and ate slowly, thinking about Karne and his enemy. He ran a fingertip over the blood-brotherhood scar, drank the last of the klag, and leaned back against the rock to See Halarek Holding and Ontar manor.

Karne was standing in the pilots' common room, examining a map pinned carelessly to the wall. Gregg, siege leader for Halarek's Specials, and Karne's other close friends among the pilots clustered around him. Karne pointed to a place in the Frozen Zone, then looked at Yan Willem, one of the Earl of Justin's nephews. "You say the Gild reports a suspicious explosion about here?"

"Yes."

"In the Frozen Zone?"

"Yes."

"Any explanation or ideas what it was or why it was?"

"Well, the Gild speaks delicately of volcanoes, but our pix experts say no, it was probably an air crash."

"No one flies over the Frozen Zone." Gregg sounded disgusted.

"That's what makes the possibility interesting," Yan said.

Karne turned to look at the stocky pilot. "You're not saying something about what you know, Yan."

"Well, it's not quite what I *know*, but my cousin's wife's brother-in-law is cousin to Lord Richard. Distant, but a cousin with the run of the manor over there. He says Natan Harlan disappeared maybe a week ago and no one's heard from him. At least publicly. Then the vassals allowed Olan to take a flitter out and he hasn't come back, either."

"Do you think Richard's killing off his brothers?"

"Natan, maybe. He's always been too ambitious for his own good, especially with Richard for an older brother. Olan? I doubt it. Richard's fond of him, if he's fond of anyone, and that old dueling injury makes him no competition for the dukedom."

Karne frowned and his hand ran back through his hair, perhaps without his awareness. "I thought Olan was an imbecile, completely incompetent, or he would never have been passed over in favor of Richard."

Yan shrugged. "Some days Olan's just as normal as everyone else. Other days he's sitting on the floor, staring at the walls for hours, or he's throwing such violent fits of temper that they lock him up." Yan pursed his lips and nodded slowly. "Come to think of it, I've been hearing lately that a small faction was pushing Olan for duke. Natan's doing, I suspect."

"A puppet for that little snake, no doubt." Dennen Willem's voice was contemptuous. "Always too big for his hosen was Natan."

There was a timid little knock at the common room door.

"Who's there?" Karne's voice had a sharp, impatient edge to it.

The answer was inaudible. Dennen Willem opened the door. A very thin, pale young woman stood hesitantly outside.

"Well?" Karne's tone was, if anything, even more impatient.

"The—the tri-d. It—the baron—an urgent message, my lord—"

Karne rounded on her. "By the Guardians, Lizanne! I don't bite."

Lizanne flinched and took a step backward. Karne muttered something harsh under his breath, then went to her, put an arm gently around her shoulders, and turned her from the room. "I'm sorry I snarled at you. It's just—we'll get used to each other's ways and, really, I'm not going to hurt you. Please believe me. Those days are over for you. Let's go see what the baron wants."

The two left the room. The pilots watched them go in silence. Finally Gregg turned away from the door with an oath. "By my mother's blood! I'll thank God every day I'm not of the Families so I don't have to get an heir on such as that!"

"She's been beaten too often, but she's not ugly and she's not infertile," Dennen Willem said grimly. "With time and patience, she may turn out all right. What advancement—

minded sire would give a daughter to a lord with the reputation Lord Karne's sire left him? Or to a lord with the Harlan
for an enemy, for that matter?"

"Lord Francis Arnette, obviously."

The laugh that followed Lord Francis's name was not a
pleasant one.

Egil came abruptly out of his trance. The ugliness of what
he had seen hung around him like a fog. He longed for the
sunshine, clear air, and clean politics of Balder. For that
moment he had a glimpse of Solveig, herself in a trance of
Seeing.

Egil spent a nearly sleepless night. He awoke before dawn
feeling restless and cranky. Harlan would take the flattest
path and Egil was at least a half a day behind him, assuming
no more traps. Egil told himself that if worse came to worst
and he could find neither the ridge nor the Ednov, he could
walk out as far as Druma and see if his father's connections
could get the Gild to show him pix of the Frozen Zone. He
would have to frame it as a personal favor toward Odin
Olafsson or the Gild would refuse on grounds of its neutrality, but—

Egil slammed one fist into the other palm. *Don't be such
a fool! Any contact with the Gharr will bring up impossible-
to-answer questions.* He bit his lip and stared into the distance. He did not like being in such a position. Once he
was free to rejoin Karne . . . He shoved the thought away.
Answers to such questions would have to wait until the more
important work was done.

Egil slid into the pack straps, took one last look toward
Halarek Holding, and swung off down the far side of the
pass.

Four days later Egil stood on the shoulder of a mountain
northeast of Druma. Twice earlier he had caught glimpses
of what he thought was Harlan, both times a dark figure
that might have been a Zinn bear, except it did not walk
like a Zinn bear and was too far from the bears' normal
range. The search seemed to go on and on. The ridge of
the Seeing had come and gone with no more sign of Harlan

than the browned grass where a thermo had sat. There had to be days of travel between that ridge and the Ednov. If it was the Ednov.

What if he's changed direction? What if I'm wrong about where he's headed? Gods, what if I don't find him again?

Thoughts of returning permanently to the Watchers drained Egil of energy. Of what value was a life away from everyone and everything he knew and loved? Egil sat down on the slope, which was green and filled with mountain wildflowers, and stared gloomily down at the settled Druma land out beyond the foothills. It was late spring or early summer and he had never seen either Aza or Verdain on Starker IV. He no longer wanted to. It had already been a long journey, and Harlan was always just ahead, just out of reach.

He could not give up now. He had found Harlan with Seeing before; he would find him the same way again if necessary. How could he feel so down when Starker IV lay green before him and the air smelled of grass and flowers and dampness and spring? On the slope below him, a grove of flowering trees seemed covered in deep red smoke. Farther down, a flock of large birds settled in the grass and began pecking at something in it. Far below that, at the foot of the mountain, on the slopes of the last of the foothills, uleks grazed. Egil could see the bright red of the herder's cloak.

See, you aren't the only human still alive. There's one down there.

But he felt like the only human. Egil stood, took one last look at the edges of civilization, and climbed the shoulder of the mountain to its other side. He did not believe Harlan would enter Druma Holding itself. He did not believe Harlan would leave the Frozen Zone. But Harlan had come close. Perhaps he had come this way for supplies, like at Breven. Perhaps he had picked up bodyguards. Perhaps Harlan just wanted a look at a holding again. He had been weeks in the wilderness, too.

Egil looked back at Druma. The Duke of Druma was an Odonnel vassal and thus a sort of ally of House Harlan, but he was also a Halarek vassal. A tough position to manage, Egil thought, caught between warring Houses by ancient promises given under very different conditions. The duke was conservative, according to what Egil had seen in Council, but the old man would not likely help a criminal, even if that criminal were a liege lord. The duke of Druma did not have that much backbone.

Harlan would go around the holding, then, taking the easiest going he could find. Egil tried to put himself in the young lord's place and could not. Harlan had wilderness knowledge, obviously, and he was hiding from assassins as well as from Council. Egil's own wilderness knowledge was Runner knowledge, which had to be very different from the knowledge of the noble classes. They were not evenly matched.

Egil climbed passes, hiked valleys, forded streams and small rivers. The sounds and scents of spring were a constant distraction from the boredom of following, following, following. Sometimes Egil wondered if he might have missed a clue, a trace, a footprint, because he was watching a bright-colored bird, or listening to insects hum in the tiny spring flowers of the mountains, or smelling the greenness of grass and leaves. Then he saw a ribbon of trail—grass bent by the passage of one, perhaps two, people—and knew he had not been too inattentive. Egil refused to let hope get very high; on the boundary of a holding, in spring, such a trail need not belong to Richard Harlan. It could belong to a shepherd. Or a hunter. Or a wild "horse" catcher. It need not be Harlan's. But it could be. Egil followed it carefully, wishing he had the Runner's experience in judging how old the trail was, or how heavy the person going over it had been, or whether the boot sole was exactly the same as the one he had been looking at much earlier in the chase.

Then he came to a cliff with new pitons still in the rock. Egil examined the pitons from the ground as best he could. Harlan had gone up this wall. Or he wanted Egil to think he had. On the other hand, the pitons could be a trap that would send Egil falling to his death.

The path was too good not to follow. Egil used the pitons,

though very carefully, and scaled the wall. It was when he was just rising to his feet after hauling himself over the top that Egil realized his mistake. At the top of such a climb, a man is defenseless. A heavy arm was around his neck and a knife pricking his belly before Egil realized he was no longer alone.

"Be you quite still, young foreigner, until my men disarm you." The deep, harsh voice held authority that brooked no challenge.

Egil heard the rustle of many men's clothing and soft, uneven breathing, as if the men had been running. The harsh voice of his captor was faintly familiar, but Egil knew no one from Druma Holding nor from any Holding but Halarek.

"Why be you here, so far from Halarek?"

The voice niggled harder at Egil's memory.

"What does it matter? I'm not hurting anything. I'm not even hunting. I'm just passing through."

"No one 'passes through' here, young foreigner. This is the Frozen Zone. It's well known no one can live here."

"But—" The arm tightened, cutting off air for speech.

Because he had a memory of that voice and the memory did not say "danger," Egil did not struggle, but allowed himself to be pushed on along the trail he had been following. He heard more pairs of feet than he could reliably count, but he was given no glimpse of either his captor or the man's companions.

Soon the trail rounded a hill and dropped into a wide basin filled with peculiar, lumpy hillocks. Steam appeared to be rising from several of these. Egil wondered for a moment if the hillocks might be part of a previously unknown thermal feature, but decided against the idea. Uleks and what looked suspiciously like goats grazed around the hillocks. *If* these were thermal features, they were not dangerous ones, Egil decided, for he had never known grazing animals to risk themselves in areas where they were likely to be sprayed with superheated steam or fall into boiling water or mud. So these had to be something else. Just as Egil came to that conclusion, he smelled woodsmoke, garlic, and cooking onions. Egil's captor let out an ear-splitting "Halooo!"

The effect was as good as a siren's. People appeared from holes in the ground and from behind rocks and out of doors in the hillocks. Thirty, perhaps forty, adults soon stood in a wary circle around Egil and his captors. They were not some exotic race, like the Watchers, as Egil had half begun to suspect his captors would be, but small, thin Gharr, thinner perhaps than was usual, even for the Gharr. Each carried a weapon—a billhook, an ax, a pitchfork, a kitchen knife, a fireplace poker—and every person looked frightened white.

"Peace, friends," said the familiar voice behind Egil. "This be not the intruder we watched for. That one traveled south of here, along the edge of Druma. You can put down your weapons."

Most in the circle did lay down their weapons, but a few did not, and from them came a murmur that might have been fear or it might have been rebellion. "Nay," said Egil's captor, "there be no punishment here for disagreement. I be no liar, but you be not required to believe me, either.

"Newcomers," the voice said quietly beside Egil's ear. "They don't trust freedom yet."

Newcomers, Egil thought. Freedom. No punishment for disagreement. That's rare, even among the noble Houses. Especially among the noble Houses.

Egil's captor relaxed until the arm across Egil's throat was merely a formality. "A moment more," the voice said beside his ear, "then I introduce you. Trust comes hard to former slaves and serfs, young foreigner."

Farm 3, Egil's memory said. You remember this voice and "young foreigner" from Farm 3. The freight lift and the smell of disinfectant and—

Egil's captor stepped out from behind him. Egil recognized Anse-the-smith, Farm 3's smith and the leader of the slave rebellion there. The smith was a squat, muscular man who had broad, uneven yellow teeth, a cagey smile, and a limp. A slave, he had been freed and made manager after the revolt at great political risk to Karne. It looked like Karne had taken the risk for nothing. This was nowhere near Farm 3.

The man motioned toward Egil. "This be a citizen of Balder, another planet such as Starker IV is. It be very, very far away. He came from his world to this one to help my master, the Lharr Halarek."

"Halarek!" many of the group whispered, as if it were a magic word.

The smith smiled. "Aye." He turned to Egil. "I had to bring you. It is the rule here. No one comes through the community without the community's knowledge. No one leaves without the community's consent. I had men with me." He motioned toward a cluster of ten or so men slightly to Egil's left rear. "I be the leader here now. I couldna break my own rules. I had to show you to them, to let them choose if you be a danger to us or not."

Egil nodded slightly to indicate his understanding. And he was just barely understanding, because the smith's accent was far from standard Rom, which was what Egil had learned in House Halarek. The meaning under the smith's words he would have to puzzle out later. If the community allowed him a later.

"You be my lord's friend, you be safe." The smith grinned suddenly, stuck his knife back into his belt, and gave Egil a sharp punch in the arm. "And if you agree to that wrestling match we talked about back at Farm 3, you'll not only leave here safe, you'll leave resupplied and with guides."

Egil relaxed and grinned back. He had caught the smith by surprise during the revolt and had made him hostage. Now the smith wanted to even things up.

"That's more than fair," Egil said. The more he thought about it, the better he liked the idea. He had often wondered how a match with the burly smith would come out. Now he could find out and have supplies and a guide to help him thrown in. With a guide who knew the territory, Harlan would be much easier to find. Egil grinned at the smith again. "In fact, I've been looking forward to such a chance for a long time." Then he sobered. The smith had talked of him as "my lord's friend," but the smith was a long, long way from Halarek Holding.

"The Lharr Halarek kept his word to you after Farm 3 and not only freed you, but made you manager of the farm. You kept your word then, but now—"

"I know what you be thinking, young foreigner. But I be a free man now, and of every ten months, I have a month of my own to do as I please. My family is here: my sons"— the smith beckoned and three boys from about four to about fifteen stepped forward out of the crowd—"and my woman, who's at home tending our new little girl. Be at ease, young foreigner. Odonnel be looking for my woman and boys still, but I be free. My lord does not care where I go. He trusts me." The smith looked directly at Egil. "Even my lord does not know of this place. I do na betray his trust by keeping silent, for my lord has no slaves anymore. I keep silence with him because my lord would believe it his duty to tell others of the Nine that their 'lost' serfs and slaves be not dead but be hiding in the Frozen Zone."

The smith did not ask for a promise of secrecy. He did not ask for an oath. He laid out briefly the facts about the people here. Egil felt the pressure of the smith's trust in him. This little community depended on him not to tell his friend or anyone else what he knew. He tried to imagine what it must be like for the smith to see his family only once a year and failed.

How much freedom must mean to him, and to his family, for them to live so much apart just to have it. How much it must mean for them to try to live in what has to be an extremely difficult climate.

Egil let his eyes roam over the new-green grass and emerald-green haystacks, the steaming hillocks, the herd of uleks and goats, the rim of ice on the nearby pond, though it was summer in the south. He could not imagine how anyone could survive year-round here, even if they had managed to dig out deep shelters, as the Freemen and the Nine had. He did not think that likely because, if they were all escapees, they had no way to get the heavy mining equipment necessary to such digging. Egil looked again at the basin and thought of the chilly mountains all around it, the icy rivers, the sun low on the horizon. Life was harsh for members of the Nine, and they lived in luxury compared to this.

Perhaps the smith guessed something of his thoughts. He cleared his throat and looked down at his feet. "If you remember, young foreigner, at the Farm I told the young Lharr I'd lost four of my toes to Odonnel's ax man for trying to escape. What I didna say was, I was bringing my wife and kids here when I was caught. They got away safe and lookouts in the hills brought them here. The lookouts find lots who'd rather die in the cold than keep on as slaves or serfs. All the serfs and slaves know these places exist, and most of the Freemen. But not the Noble Nine, thank the Guardians!" The smith looked up with a grin. "Odonnel took my toes, young foreigner, but don't count on that bein' much help to you in our match. I've had many years to get used to bein' without them." The smith slung an arm over Egil's shoulders. "Say he can go on his way, people, and then he can stay for supper."

The circle of people gave one glad shout and then returned to whatever they had been doing when the smith announced their arrival. The smith led Egil around one of the hillocks, opened a heavy door there, and motioned Egil inside.

The hillock was really a combination communal house and barn. It was dome-shaped and made of logs about a meter long laid up like a woodpile and caulked and mortared with what smelled like mud and manure. Each family had private quarters marked off with opaque woven screens that cut off sight but let air through. Though the air had been nippy outside, inside it was both warm and humid.

The smith waved one hand toward the other end of the building. "The animals are out to pasture now, as you probably saw, but they spend the winter in here and no one needs to go out into the cold. It's shirt-warm in here, my wife says."

Egil thought he heard a trace of longing in the smith's voice, for of course he could not be away from the farm an entire winter and, once Uhl came, he could not leave at all. Egil tried again to imagine what it must be like to be separated from one's family for all but one month a year and never to be able to talk to anyone about them, because they were supposedly dead of exposure. He shook himself. His separation from his own family had been voluntary, at least until he ran into the Watchers.

CHAPTER 10

Anse-the-smith led Egil to his family's quarters, where his wife had a meal waiting. Egil was given the place of honor at the head of the narrow, battered table and a seat on the only chair. The smith's wife offered him a steaming heap of some stringy meat Egil guessed was goat; the oldest son filled a mug with something that smelled strongly alcoholic; the youngest son brought him plate and basket and cloth, each full of vegetables. The family sat on benches at the sides of the table and watched him eat. The moment he finished his serving of meat, the wife offered more. The oldest son kept the mug filled with what turned out to be quite decent beer. Egil felt extremely uncomfortable about the deference and finally deciding he was a proxy for Karne did not help much. He ate lightly, figuring that there was not really food to spare: He had not seen even one plump person since his arrival. As if to confirm his surmise, the smith's family did not eat until he had finished.

The meal finally over, Egil expected to be challenged to a match, but the smith instead took him on a tour of the village. Slowly Egil began to understand the drive and ingenuity required to live in a place where the ground was always frozen a foot below the surface, where there were no trees, where all food had to be grown indoors, and where grain, when there was any, had to be stolen from the holdings. The only electricity was used for running the 'ponics sheds and the fuel for that was pirated cleverly from the lines running between Druma and the minor holding of House Konnor. Household illumination was by tallow candle, and that meant that people went to bed early and slept long, especially in winter.

The smith took a candle and led Egil down a short stair to a heavily insulated door. The smith shoved open the door and waited for Egil's reaction. The door opened into a tunnel hacked from the permafrost. The tunnel was more than man-high and speckled with ice crystals, probably condensed from the breath of people passing through. There was no shoring or support of other sort and none was needed: The ground was permanently frozen hard as stone. Egil's response was only a sharp intake of breath in surprise and admiration, but it was apparently enough. The smith smiled and led the way down the tunnel. Egil followed, trailing a finger through the feathers of ice on the tunnel walls as he passed, in awe of the accomplishment and thinking how different Starker IV would have been if the Watchers had discovered such ideas in their first years on this world.

"This tunnel be to one of the 'ponics sheds," the smith said. "There be others to all the other buildings. Like a maze they be, sort of, but everyone gets to know them in time."

The smith followed a left-branching tunnel and opened a door at its end with considerable pride. The 'ponics shed contained row after row of 'ponics tables, each full of colored nutrient solutions and the vegetables they nourished. There were deep windows facing south to catch what sun there was and deep plugs to fill the windows to keep out cold and snow in winter rested against inside walls. The windows themselves were glazed with translucent plastic, stolen from some lord's manor conservatory. Any lord would have been proud of such a clean, well-managed shed. Of course, 'ponics was what the smith managed for Karne at Farm 3. The smith pointed out doors to other tunnels and other buildings.

"We don't go outside in winter no more than the lords do. It's not a bad life, young foreigner."

Again Egil felt the smith's unspoken urging to keep this hideaway secret. He wondered if the urging would become a demand before he was allowed to leave. He hoped not. He had had enough oaths and the problems they caused already.

They left the shed by a stair and an exterior door. "They sink into the frost, you know," the smith offered as the two men climbed the stair. "The buildings, I mean. Another ten years or so and we'll be walking *up* to reach the tunnels."

They emerged into twilight and the sounds of the animals being driven into their barns for milking and the night. The uleks came slowly, chewing their cuds, gazing with rather stupid eyes at first this side of their route and then the other. The goats in their thick, shaggy coats came in fits and starts, maaing, leaping, butting heads, some looking anxiously for kids and calling, some deciding to stop where they were. The animals crowded through the doors into the barns and were shut in for the night.

"Hogs stay inside all the time," the smith said. "No fur."

The men walked slowly back to the smith's house. The village was very quiet. A faint haze rose from the pines. Its tangy scent mingled pleasantly with the smell of wood-smoke. Anse stopped in the house's doorway. He studied the graying skyline.

"I said once I wanted to fight you, young foreigner. I still do. But not for harm. A test of skills only. But I don't want to delay you overmuch, either, because your goal is my goal. I know you be not here by getting lost hunting or being driven off a holding to die. I suspect you be *hunting*, all right, though not exactly animals. We've watched the would-be lord of Harlan pass by on the edge of Druma these last five days. That's important prey, but not for the likes of us. I won't cause you to lose him."

Egil looked off in the same direction and grimaced rue-fully. "I've lost him already."

The smith nodded slowly, his eyes still on the horizon. "I thought so. You be too far off his trail. Yet you wouldn't be after him if you weren't my lord's friend. Be that also right?"

"Yes." *Heimdal, the man's smart!*

The smith turned and looked up at Egil. "Then I'll strike another bargain with you, different from the one I said at first. I get a fair match with you and not for harm. Done tomorrow so as not to slow you down. In return, you get resupplied as best we can and get a guide and several fighters to take you to the Harlan. Is it a bargain?"

"What do you mean by 'resupplied,' and how far will these people go with me?"

"I mean dried meat, a little beer, a charge or two for your stunner, if we have two, and six or seven men and women who know the land as far as the Ednov."

Egil thrust out his hand, then remembered that only the Families shook hands on this world and then only on ceremonial occasions. He stuck his hand back into his pocket and let his voice speak his enthusiasm and agreement. "It's a bargain, and heavily in my favor, I think."

The smith looked up at him and then back at the horizon. "That depends, young foreigner, on how much winning means to you."

Egil shrugged and shivered and laughed and turned toward the house, suddenly aware that he was outside in the cold night air without even a sweater to keep him warm. "Winning? I value winning. But there's not a lot that's worth as much to me as getting quickly on Harlan's trail again. And I didn't wear my parka outside." He ducked under the door and into the domed house.

The smith followed. "Cold, soft-climate man?"

"My name's Egil, Egil Olafsson. And yes."

The smith chuckled, slapped Egil's shoulder, and led him back to his family's quarters, where the wife and children had rolled out mattresses and bedding. After the younger children had been put to bed, the adults and the oldest son sat around the table drinking beer and exchanging stories. They set the match time for shortly after dawn, so Egil could travel—"if he be able," the smith teased—in the warmest hours of the day.

They talked late and morning came too soon for Egil, awakened by the sounds in the huge house. People talked beyond the partitions. They spoke very quietly, but there

were so many that they still made a murmur of conversation
that was loud enough to be disturbing to one who had spent
many nights in the heavy quiet of caves. There were also the
morning sounds of any household, multiplied by the many
families living in this one. Anse-the-smith was already up
and drinking a cup of klag.

"Be you ready, young foreigner?" The smith looked at
Egil assessingly over the edge of his cup. "The ring be
ready."

Egil nodded. "I'm ready."

"You be wanting food first?"

The table had been shoved against a partition for the night.
It now had on it a loaf of coarse bread, a hunk of dark goat
cheese, and cups for klag. Egil looked at the food and then
at the smith. This could be a tradition of hospitality here,
or it could be a sly way for the smith to gain an advantage
in the match. No one fought well on a full stomach. Egil
decided to chance being rude. He shook his head.

"Let's go, then."

Egil knew from the way the smith's eyes slid away from
his that the offer of food had been a test. And that he had
passed it. He followed the smith out into the icy predawn
air. A square had been made with stakes and rope. The ring
was behind the smith's home and very close to the edge of
the clearing it sat in. It was Egil's guess that the ring must
be a permanent feature, both because he doubted that stakes
could be driven into the permafrost more than two or three
months of the year and because the ring was set up out of
the way of general village traffic.

The smith lifted a rope and motioned Egil inside. Villagers followed and soon filled the open area outside the
ring. The smith motioned to a plump, fiftyish woman, who
ducked under the rope and came to him.

The smith looked at Egil, then set his hand on the woman's shoulder. "This is Marta. She'll be the judge or referee,
whichever you call it in your world."

Marta assessed Egil silently for a long-drawn-out moment, nodded, then waved her hand around the roped-in
area. "All moves be made within the ropes. If you leave

by your own act, even so much as a foot leaves the ring, you have lost."

Sort of like the *holmganga*, Egil thought, only this is not for blood.

"Neither of you will use killing holds," Marta went on. "No body breaking, no making eyes nor ears nor crotches targets. There will be no attacks once a man is down or pinned. A win means two points of the opponent's body is held to the ground to a count of thirty. Is that agreed?"

The two men nodded.

"Then let the contest begin." Marta backed out of the ring.

The smith stripped down to a breechclout. Egil swallowed, shivered, and did the equivalent. His skin tightened taut as a drumhead, in the cold. It was so taut he could not shiver. It was so cold the smith's first rush almost caught him by surprise. Egil leaped out of the way at the last moment. He spun, lunged forward, caught the smith, and began bending him forward in the *kalid*. The smith dropped to the ground. Egil tumbled after, off balance, and the smith pinned one of his shoulders in seconds. Egil heaved upward, counting off the time in his head. The smith held him down with ease and began pressing the other shoulder toward the ground.

For a moment Egil's mind went blank with astonishment. The contest could not end so quickly. He was a district Drinn champion! The smith pressed harder, shifting weight of necessity. Egil let himself go loose for a fraction of a second. The smith's weight shifted more than the man expected because the resistance was gone and with that shift Egil threw himself toward the shoulder the smith was leaning on. The smith rolled onto his side. Egil threw his weight over the smith and applied a *kronwa* to his lower body. The smith twisted and reared upward. Egil tightened the *kronwa* and grabbed the smith's arm as it came round his neck. But Egil could not keep the arm off, he could only keep it from tightening.

The two men rolled around the ring, one struggling to apply a stranglehold, the other resisting with all his power.

Sweat slickened Egil's body and the smith's. Spots of frost shocked Egil's hot skin as they rolled over the grass.

The smith's arm tightened bit by bit. Both men panted and dripped sweat. Egil managed to hold the smith's back to the ground, but only to a count of fifteen. The smith heaved over, pressing Egil against the icy ground. Egil writhed and twisted and broke free. The smith lunged upward and caught Egil in a bear hug. Egil pressed his hands hard against the smith's elbows, shoved upward, and slid down the smith's body at the same time, using their sweat as lubricant. He was out of the hold and lurching backward in order to get a breath. The smith threw himself at Egil. They both went down in a tangle of limbs and definitely unorthodox holds. Egil heard the referee step into the ring and come closer and somewhere in the back of his mind, he knew she was checking for illegal moves, but the smith was fighting hard and fair and just staying out of pins took most of Egil's attention.

The man's good. Very, very good, Egil thought.

In that second of divided attention, the smith flipped Egil onto his back. Egil used his legs to lever the man onto his side, but he could not get the smith's uppermost shoulder to move even a millimeter toward the ground.

The battle continued until neither man could move for weariness. The smith sat on Egil's waist, but did not have the strength to press both shoulders to the ground. Egil had only enough strength to keep the second shoulder millimeters from touching; he had no strength to throw the man off. Finally the smith rolled off and lay flat on his back beside Egil.

"Young foreigner, it be more than twenty years since I've had such a fight as this, and that one I finally won."

For a time the only sounds were the gasping breaths of the two wrestlers and the muted whispers of the spectators. Then Marta came and stood over them.

"Are you finished? Fight you more?"

The two men rolled their heads toward each other, exchanged looks, and laughed.

"Want you a judgment on technical points?"

The men shook their heads.

"Then I say this is a draw and neither man need feel the shame of a loss." Marta gathered her layers of skirts in one hand, stepped over the smith's feet, and left the ring.

Late in the afternoon of the same day, Egil's guide, a gaunt young woman with a babyboard on her back, motioned him to join her at the curve in the shoulder of the mountain they had been climbing for the past two hours. Below, the river ran between the mountains. Eons before, a glacier had carved out the strip down which the river now flowed. The mountain on which Egil stood sloped rather gently down to the floodplain. The river, wide and slow here, filled most of the valley with water and marsh. A crane stood motionless in the reeds on the river's far side. A wom doe came out of the trees beyond the crane, saw the people high on the mountain opposite, and bounded away as if the grass had suddenly burst into flame in front of her.

"Wom," said the woman for the foreigner's benefit. Her contempt for the creature showed in her voice. She pointed northeast, which was upstream. "You're as far south on the river as we dared come. Because of the holdings. Harlan couldn't have been south of here, anyway, not if he crossed at the rocky place you describe."

She adjusted the position of the babyboard a trifle, said something caressing to the baby, and walked toward the river without a backward glance for the rest of her party.

The river continued to be broad and slow and marshy for some distance upstream; Egil and his companions camped two nights on fringes of marshes. By the third night the river had narrowed and flowed swiftly. Egil's hopes rose. The water's speed was now much like what he had Seen. But the banks were not yet right. Here they were barely above water level and gravelly.

The guide, whose name was Rez, ordered guards posted that night and set them in four-hour shifts. Egil took an early shift. Later, when he should have been sleeping soundly, he heard guards walking quietly past several times. The sounds left him with an uneasy feeling.

In the morning, Rez reported one of the till-dawn guards had disappeared. The best trackers in the group searched for half the morning, but they found only a stranger's footprints leading westward back into the mountains and those footprints soon vanished on a long strip of smooth rock.

"Slave hunter, probably," Rez said. "Crossed our trail somehow farther south and followed, waiting his chance. Alla was from House Konnor once. That's why he was along, because he ran from there through here and knew this part of the river." She looked at the faces of her neighbors. "Check your weapons," she said. "Load them if they have ammunition. Be sure the edges are sharp otherwise. You may not have time to do it later."

Egil doubted the slave-hunter idea, but he said nothing in front of the group. Later he asked Rez what a slave hunter would be doing in the Frozen Zone where no one went. She shook her head. She did not want to think about it, let alone talk about it, but she did keep the group closer together as they hiked north. No one went out of sight, even on private business. No one went hunting. Few felt like talking.

Egil wished for a short time alone to do a Seeing, but Rez would not have allowed that, so he did not bother to ask. She was right. The risk of being alone and unprotected when a stranger was nearby was too great. Rez's caution made Egil realize how much he had come to depend on the hints and little tidbits of important information a Seeing so often gave him. He would have to puzzle this situation out without that help.

If slave hunters come here, no villager is safe, Egil thought. *These people have already paid a very high price to be free. Facing the idea of slave hunters in what they thought was safe territory . . .* Egil shook his head. *These aren't, usually, educated people. They know even less of Starker's geography than I do. They know only their own neighborhoods.*

The guard who had disappeared had been brought because he knew the land in this particular area. Each member of the little group had probably been included for the same reason. They knew how unlikely it would be for a slave hunter—who would be a Freeman or a younger son of a very minor House—to come into a territory in which, Gharr nobles and Freemen knew, no one and nothing lived. No, the intruder might or might not be involved with the guard's disappearance, but he was not a slave hunter. Egil wished again for a quiet place and enough time for a Seeing.

At noon the group came to the tumbled rocks of Egil's vision. There was no sign of human passing on or around the rocks. Egil wanted to cross at once, but three of the group wanted to go back. They had come far enough from home, they said.

"There'll be no guide back," Rez told them. "We promised Anse to see this foreigner as far as he needed to go." As if to make her point, Rez checked the security of the baby's moorings, then stepped out onto the rocks. No one left.

Rez must have heard a noise, because she dropped to the rocks. A yellow tracer sizzled through the air where she had just been. The villagers scattered like chickens before a hawk.

"Now we know where the guard went," Egil snarled as he, too, ducked behind the nearest large rock.

Rez lay very still, but the baby, terrified by the suddenness of the drop, was screaming. Egil watched and tried to think of something to do to help. Rez was the best target around at the moment and she had come with him to help. This wasn't her fight, it was Egil's and Karne's!

Suddenly enraged by the underhandedness of a spy even among these poor refugees, Egil stood with a roar and swept the rocks across the river with his stunner on "high." "Run, Rez!" With all the rock, the sniper was not likely to be hurt, but he was likely to be numb just long enough for Rez and her baby to get to cover. "Run!" he repeated, and sprayed the rocks again.

The woman rose to a crouch, whipped the babyboard off her back and around in front of her, and ran zigzagging toward the large rock where Egil stood. The yellow of beamer bolts and the wider, blue stripes of stunner fire, from a different place, followed her. It wasn't just Harlan across the river, then. Egil looked for the source of the beamer fire. One of the villagers stood quickly and fired an antique percussion weapon toward the rocks where the stunner had been. Chips of rock flew. A stunner fired back from a third position. The villager crumpled to the ground. Another villager crawled to the dead man and dragged him and his weapon out of sight. Egil glanced at Rez. She had the now-quiet baby off the board and was rapidly checking his body for injuries. Egil wondered briefly what she had done to silence the child, for on Balder babies cried until they felt like stopping, no matter what adults tried to do to quiet them.

Egil heard a choked cry from another of the villagers, then the clitter of rocks sliding and the sounds of fists into bodies. A rock tumbled over others on the bank behind. Egil spun. A soldier in Odonnel's black and white checks was catching his balance and cursing the rock, just within range. Egil shot him. The man fell and his beamer tumbled down the bank and into the river. *We're surrounded,* Egil thought, *and by a number of men.*

He turned at a muffled sound from Rez. She was fighting an Odonnel man twice her weight who appeared to be trying to step on the baby.

Baby's not worth a beamer bolt to him, apparently, Egil thought.

Egil dodged this way and that, looking for a chance to shoot without hurting Rez. If it hadn't been for the baby, he would have stunned them both, then finished off the Odonnel man, but he remembered how close he had come to killing Skadi and her sister with a charge that did not faze their mother. No, the baby couldn't take the energy necessary to put an adult out.

The Odonnel man forgot about the baby and turned his attention to keeping Rez between himself and Egil's stunner while he struggled to get his own beamer arm out of Rez's grip. The woman was taking a terrible beating, but she was preventing the man from shooting anything useful to him. Then, in a movement almost too quick to see, she leaned into the man, snatched his belt knife from its sheath, plunged the blade into his side, and ripped upward. The man looked astonished, then his hands dropped away from her and he felt his side. He looked at his bloody fingers and then stared at Rez with a mixture of hate and terror. Rez tore the beamer from his hand, spun, and turned it on the men coming over the rocks on the other side of the river.

Egil came to himself with a start. He had been staring like a beginner while Rez turned her back on a wounded enemy, but then she was not a trained warrior. Egil shot the Odonnel man with stunner on "high," to be sure the man was dead, then, with flying fingers, Egil tied the baby back on the board, set the board upright against the rock so the baby would be out of sight and harm's way both, then returned to the fight. He fired at a checked uniform that was tying the arms of one of the villagers behind her; the soldiers would not have a merciful reason for sparing the woman's life.

Egil stared at the rocks across the river, from which beamer bolts were still coming. How many soldiers were there? How had they known Egil and his crew were coming? How had they known where to wait? A beamer sizzled over the top of the rock, singeing the fur on Egil's parka hood. Egil ducked and looked around the side of the rock. Both sides had plenty of shelter. Anywhere else that people still had wars, the fight could have turned quickly into a standoff, with minimum casualties until one side's food or water ran out, but the Gharr soldier expected to leave secure shelter— his underground manor house or barracks—and fight, so that's what the Odonnel men were doing. The serfs had not been raised to that code, however. Already the firing from both sides was sparser. A beamer bolt sizzled, someone screamed in pain, then the firing ceased. Egil pulled Rez fully into the shelter of the rock and motioned her to stay still. He noticed her face was contorted with extreme fear or rage and tears wet her cheeks. She picked up the baby, cradled him board and all against her chest, and rested her head against his.

Egil waited several minutes. Nothing happened. He examined every tree and rock at his back. There was no movement there, no sound that did not belong to the river and the mountains. He looked around the base of the rock. Four Odonnel men and two villagers lay sprawled on the rocks. None of them moved. One of the bodies was the bound woman. Egil waited some more, then he crept on his belly from behind the rock, wishing for the first time in his life that he were a much smaller man, and examined the bodies. Five were dead. The bound woman whimpered. Egil untied her and pointed toward the rock where Rez waited. The woman rose to a low crouch and ran. No one fired at her.

Egil risked rising to his haunches. No reaction from the enemy. He stood in a crouch. Still no reaction. It could be sadism on the part of the remaining Odonnel men. If there were any remaining Odonnel men. Egil stood and looked over the battleground. A couple squads of soldiers, maybe. The villagers had sold their lives high. Egil felt a sudden ache in the pit of his stomach. The fight had not been theirs. They had come to help because their leader had ordered them to and their leader had done that because his lord had been, by the standards of Starker IV, unbelievably good to him. Perhaps, in the depths of his heart, the smith held the dream that someday he could tell his lord about his family and bring them to his home to live. Perhaps.

Egil found three more dead villagers and counted fifteen Odonnel bodies. If there had been more soldiers, they had either gone or were lying very low. He went back to the rock and the women. He called Rez's attention from the baby by touching her shoulder lightly. "Take whatever food the others had in their packs, Rez, and the two of you go back to the village. The river's edge was the boundary of your agreement and you've kept that agreement in blood. I think these men meant to find me alone and kill me, so their lord could run free to the protection of his friends. I live because your neighbors died protecting me. Go home. You've done more than I meant to ask of you." He looked at Rez. "You were brave beyond my understanding of women."

The woman met his eyes and inclined her head in regal recognition, then returned her attention to checking and rechecking the baby, assuring herself again and again that the child was unhurt.

CHAPTER 11

Egil watched the women until they disappeared beyond a ridge, then he turned and cautiously crossed the jumble of rocks that bridged the river and climbed the steep bank on the other side. Behind the bank top, in the shelter of overhanging rocks, lay nightbags, spare parkas, boxes of ammunition. He salvaged a stunner and two power packs for it and dropped them over his shoulder into his pack. They hadn't put up tents. Did that mean they hadn't been by the river long? Maybe they had not been laying an ambush. Maybe his arrival had surprised them and they had attacked to protect Harlan's identity.

Egil followed a trail churned into the gravel and small rocks to a grove of trees well back from the river. Here was where they had built warming fires or cooked, because Egil smelled the thick, throat-closing smell of doused fires. Egil set his stunner control to down but not kill an attacker and followed the smell. He reached a small clearing and saw the source of the fire smell. There had been a fire. The villager guard who had disappeared lay near it on his face, dead, a checked parka clenched in his right hand, his left hand burned almost off. He had been tortured in other ways, too.

Poor devil, Egil thought. *That's how Harlan found out where I'd be.*

The unfortunate villager might also have been tortured into revealing his village's existence, but only if Harlan had some reason to think the man was not Halarek property. Egil considered the self-certainty rampant among Gharr aristocracy. Harlan wouldn't even consider the possibility that such an "obvious" conclusion about a serf was merely an assumption; it would be fact in his eyes. What other reason would a serf have for being in the Frozen Zone, if not to protect his master? All the man's capture had probably done for Harlan, besides giving him a good ambush location, was to reassure him that his pursuers were not from Council.

Egil rolled the dead man over with his foot. Under him, pressed flat and damp from the frozen earth, was a map. The map had been hand-drawn, carefully, on sturdy paper. A dark line led from the Zone north of Breven along the rim of the volcanic area, through the mountains, and just over the border of Druma Holding. Some lines had been added in red-brown ink instead of the black of the original. The new lines marked out a basin east of Ednov, a basin that appeared to cover an area the size of Halarek and von Schuss Holdings combined. It was labeled in crooked letters, "geysers." A wavy line, as if the hand drawing it were very weak or very tired, crossed the basin at an angle, from the Ednov southeastward toward Council ground and the York.

"Interesting. What protection will Harlan find in that neighborhood?" For perhaps the hundredth time since he climbed the mountains beyond the Place of Leaving, Egil wished he knew more about Starker's geography and politics, especially its alliances.

Egil looked more closely at the dead man. A short, pointed stick rested in one of the parka's folds, a stick with a red-brown point. Egil looked more carefully at the dead man. A dark, beaded line crossed the veins of his lower left arm, not far above the charring. "Heimdal! After what had already been done to him, he made such a choice!"

Harlan must have left the camp long enough for the villager to draw in the new lines on the map, which he had gotten out of the parka. He had drawn the new line, then hidden the map under him. Egil shook his head, not understanding such courage or such loyalty to a leader. In the first

Viking Age, perhaps, his people had understood such. Not now. The man had cut himself, when he must have already been in agony and at the edge of deep shock . . .

Egil folded the map carefully and stuck it into an outside pocket of his pack. He resolved that somehow, if he survived to reach civilization again, this villager's courage would be recognized.

"I'm going to bury this one," Egil muttered. "He deserves that much."

Egil composed the villager's body, cringing as he of necessity touched the destroyed hand, and piled a mound of rocks over the body. He stepped back and looked at the pile. He spoke in the ritual rhythms of worship, though not the ritual words, for this man of another faith.

"I give you not a ship burial, stranger-friend," he said, "but a place to hide, protected from wolves. Rest in peace till Ragnarok, in which future may you fight at my side."

He stayed a moment longer, offering a prayer such as the followers of The Way sometimes did, just to be sure the man's spirit had whatever comfort the gods of both worlds could offer, then he turned quickly away and cast around for a trail. When he found it, it was pointed east-southeast, in the direction of the red-brown line on the map. Harlan had laid his trap of Odonnel men and left.

Three days later, Egil looked down into the geyser basin. Mist thinned and thickened over it. Its surface, where it could be seen, was bright yellow, striped and swirled with white and orange and cream. It looked granular where dry, shiny where wet, and it lay in a narrow oval between the Ednov valley and the mountains to the south, the mountains that led to House Konnor and Gildport and another Retreat House and the freecity of Neeran. Again Egil wondered what the Harlan Heir could be running to in that unfriendly neighborhood. Almost directly south of where Egil stood, and across the geyser basin's long western end, was a narrow pass through the mountains, Harlan's goal, surely, where he could have free run of the steppes and plains to the south. As if to confirm Egil's deduction, a human figure moved rapidly southward through the center of the geyser basin.

"Harlan," Egil whispered.

He started down into the basin, looking and listening carefully before each step, using rocks and bushes for cover when there were any. Occasionally he tossed a rock ahead where he suspected a pit trap. But there were no traps. Apparently Harlan had been sure the soldiers would be enough. They would have been enough against one man.

About halfway into the basin, Egil heard a faint whistling. Looking around, Egil saw a tiny trickle of steam floating from a hole not a meter from his feet. He leaped away, just in the nick of time: A steam geyser blew, shooting steam horizontally for several hundred meters. Egil let out a little sigh of relief. That had been close! He walked down to the floor of the basin even more carefully, avoiding areas that had the slightest suggestion of granulation or wetness. Better safe than not, he told himself.

Egil stopped on level ground and assessed his situation. Two geysers spouted at brief intervals just ahead of him. The ground around them would most likely be thin and treacherous. A geyser to the north blew off continuously with a roar, like steam from a broken pipe. In some places hot water came to the surface in deep, dark-blue pools. In other places, water burbled through tiny holes in the surface, blowing tiny bubbles, or came up through equally hot mud that bubbled and popped ominously. Sometimes the heat escaped as only a roar or a loud whistling. The basin was a noisy place. That was an advantage.

Egil pulled out the map and studied the wavering line, looked at the basin, studied the line again. He walked along the edge of the basin until he crossed Harlan's tracks. There, after a moment's thought about that cousin on Balder, he took his first, careful step onto the surface of the basin itself. This part would be hard, because there was no cover but mist and steam.

Though he could not see Harlan at the moment and had only tracks to follow, Egil's confidence rapidly increased. He had been lucky earlier, on the mountain, when the sun had penetrated the mist and helped him see the figure below. It was unlikely Harlan could have seen him. In addition to this luck, Harlan seemed to have a secure path. Egil saw no mistakes, no slight accidental stepping into hot mud, no cracking of a fragile surface by a hapless foot. Egil began to trot along Harlan's trail, then to lope. Steam concealed him most of the time, so he could quickly catch up. Whenever the veil of steam thinned, Egil slowed and looked for Harlan. If he could see so much as a shadow of him, he waited until Harlan was again hidden by mist before moving forward. They were about three-fourths of the way across the basin now and Egil was close enough to hear Harlan's footsteps.

Egil realized mist carried sound better than clear air, but he drew his stunner, anyway. By the time he saw Harlan, it might be too late to pull the weapon. He looked at the stunner's charge. The ambush had really drawn it down and the renewal cartridge was in the backpack. This would have to do, though, because the rustling and clinking of taking off the pack would betray his position to Harlan immediately. He only intended to stun him long enough to tie his hands and put a lead on him, but Harlan would not know that. Harlan would see Karne Halarek's blood brother, bent on vengeance.

Suddenly Egil realized he was not hearing Harlan's footsteps anymore. He froze and listened. Toward the center of the basin, a geyser rumbled, then went off with an explosive roar. Nearby, a vent hissed. Water, probably boiling hot, trickled over rocks. Egil took a tentative step forward, avoiding anything on the ground that would make a sound. He heard nothing. Egil waited. He heard only the sounds of the basin. He sank into a crouch; if he had to wait until Harlan made a move, he might as well rest his legs and back.

Again, his luck was with him. Something made a pale sizzling sound where his head had been moments before. *Heimdal! A stunner! He's within range!* Egil thought of lying flat and rejected the idea, because, flat, he would be helpless if Harlan were really close. He duck-walked as close to the edge of the solid-looking ground as he dared and waited. Another shot sizzled through the mist, higher.

An exaggerated idea of how tall I am, obviously. Egil tried to remember if Harlan had ever seen him and could not. Perhaps he had other exaggerated ideas, too.

Egil heard a slight crunching, the sound of someone walking on the mineral sprayed all over the basin's surface. He held his breath. A vent beside him hissed. Egil listened harder over the noise. Perhaps the crunching was still going on; he could no longer be sure. A geyser erupted with rhythmic *whoosh, swish, swish, swish*, a set of sounds Egil recognized from Balder as a geyser with a tall central flume and then much smaller eruptions, like ruffles around the central flume's base. The noise masked whatever sounds Harlan was making. As a precaution, Egil moved back to the trail, but two meters from where he had been.

Nothing happened for a short time, then footsteps crunched rapidly away. Harlan was leaving as fast as he dared. Egil stood carefully, waited, then followed Harlan's tracks toward the edge of the basin, stunner ready.

Egil saw the two rows of skid marks and realized too late he had been tricked. A hot puff of sulphur-scented air warned him he was too close to a pool, then Egil saw the deep-blue water. Its surface bubbled and began to surge. Egil spun and ran. The granular surface under his feet crunched, cracked, and began to sink. Egil looked wildly for the trail he had been following and leaped back toward it. Harlan came out of the mist, stunner in hand. Steaming mud oozed up through the cracks around Egil's feet. Egil fired. Harlan swore as his stunner fell from his hand, its beam sinking harmlessly into the ground. Egil's feet burned, even through the thick soles of his boots. He lunged onto more secure ground. Harlan's hand darted toward Egil's stunner and wrenched at it. Egil's hand did not have the strength to hold on. The gun fell into the blue pool with a splat. Harlan lunged for the stunner on the ground. Egil kicked it. It, too, landed in the deep-blue pool, where it sank with a thick gurgle. Both men watched it sink with dismay.

Harlan recovered first. He swore, whirled, and kicked. Egil twisted sideways; the kick landed on the meat of his inner thigh, neither where nor with the power Harlan had intended. Egil grabbed Harlan's foot. Harlan flailed for balance. The blue pool heaved ominously. Harlan lurched forward and chopped at Egil's wrists. Egil's hands did not have the strength to hold on against such a blow, so Harlan twisted free and ran. Egil followed. The pool heaved. Egil ran faster. The pool heaved again and a fountain geyser leaped upward with its characteristic *whoosh*. Scalding-hot water pattered down. Harlan, only narrowly ahead, swore steadily.

Swish, swish, swish. WHOOSH! Hot droplets burned Egil's cheeks and the backs of his hands. Just ahead were the pale green leaves and grass and the gravelly slope of one of the southern mountains. Harlan scrabbled up the slope on all fours, still swearing. He was just out of reach. Ignoring the scalding water, Egil scrambled after him. The other man's smaller size and weight were clearly an advantage to him. He was definitely pulling away. Egil cursed himself for wanting to use the last shots in the stunner before changing the power pack.

Harlan reached the beginning of the pass and some kind of trail, for he stood and ran. In perhaps a quarter of an hour, he was out of sight. When Egil reached the top of the pass, he saw mountains stretching to his right and left as far as he could see. Directly ahead and below, the mountains and the rolling land beyond were black with pines. Harlan himself was nowhere in sight.

Harlan could hide an army in there and no one would see them, Egil thought. *I wouldn't stand a chance.*

He looked at the game trail that wound down the south side of the pass. That was where Harlan probably had gone. He had taken the easy path, whenever there was one, every time so far. But to continue pursuit now was too much. He had traveled hard and fought hard. He thought with a shudder of slipping deeper and deeper into the boiling mud, his muscles cooking off his bones.

And fear takes a lot out of a man. Tired as I am, to chase Harlan into those trees, where he might have an army waiting . . . I couldn't be alert enough to survive.

A warm damp wind blew down the pass. Egil selected a site out of the wind, so the tent would not snap and pop constantly, and sheltered from passing eyes by pines and low, leafy shrubs. He set up the tent, crawled into his sleeping bag, and was almost instantly asleep.

CHAPTER 12

The next morning, Egil found Harlan's trail easily in the longish grass that grew farther down the pass. His enemy was still alone, but among the trees Harlan would have lots of cover and now he knew for certain he was being pursued and by whom. Egil took the Odonnel stunner from his pack, struck camp, and followed the trail. He felt relatively safe on the slope, because Harlan would have to leave the cover of trees to come within range to use any weapon. Just short of the tree line, Egil stopped, suddenly uneasy. The first trees were the scrawny, distorted dwarfs common to high elevations and cold places. It was most unlikely that Harlan could have found a hiding place among them. Still, Harlan was a native of this world and had clearly studied this area as best he could before his escape. He had the native's advantage. And there was something dangerous going on: The trail was too easy to follow. Egil's hand tightened on the stunner and he studied the path of bent grass intently, his mind racing.

If Harlan were trying to shake pursuit, he asked himself, *wouldn't he walk on rock outcroppings as much as he could? Wouldn't he look for the least fragile of the plants so as to leave the least mark? I don't like situations where the advantage can shift from the hunter to the hunted in a moment. If only I had Gorm with me! Gorm would sniff Harlan out.* But Gorm was back on Balder, probably sleeping on an old rug somewhere in the house.

Egil checked the stunner's power pack, then, holding the stunner in his right hand, its safety off, its firing mechanism on "wait," he cautiously entered the first cluster of trees. The trees were barely as tall as Egil, bent, twisted pines that clung to the rocks with gnarled roots. The wind soughed through the tiny needles. The sound was small and lonely. Egil's own feet seemed to make unbelievably loud crunchings and gratings on the stiff little plants and sharp gravel underfoot. Even the high-pitched warning whistle of some sort of alpine rodent seemed meant for him. He told himself the animal was only warning its community of an intruder, but he was not really sure he was the intruder the animal saw. Egil felt like a very large target.

Harlan could hear me clear down at the bottom, he thought with annoyance. *Of course, there's no sneaking up on him anymore, anyway. He knows I'm here. He can pick a hiding place and snipe. He can attack from ambush. He can have arranged for more bodyguards.*

Egil cursed himself for the pride that had kept him from capturing Harlan that first day. If only he had looked ahead that night, he would have Seen that one chance was his only chance. But Harlan had had as good a chance of killing Egil as Egil had had of taking Harlan. What help would a dead friend have been to Karne? And he was back to the old circular arguments.

Egil proceeded with extreme caution, knowing that caution was slowing him a lot, knowing without it he might be slowed permanently. Or he might not. Harlan might have only run and left no traps.

The farther down the mountain Egil went, the taller and thicker the trees. He stopped frequently to look around him and to listen. He felt exposed, as he had not on the open slopes, where he could at least have seen his enemy. By midmorning, the sun had warmed the pine needles, which filled the air with their green, pitchy scent. On Egil's left, a brook gurgled. In the trees squirrels chattered and birds rustled and murmured. Perhaps the hand of the god was still on him and had given him luck. Perhaps Harlan had such a lead that pursuit no longer mattered to him.

A flock of birds rose from the trees to his right with a frightened squawking. A moment later a great numbness swept across Egil and he sank to the ground. *Harlan! He had a spare weapon, too.* Egil had enough sense of touch left to catch himself, so the fall did not break anything, and to roll onto his back so he could breathe.

Egil assessed his situation in a flash. He was not dead. He was not even unconscious. He just could no longer move. Why hadn't Harlan killed him? Did he think to torture information out of him? Not likely. Egil knew nothing useful to a lord of the Gharr. The incongruity bothered Egil. Why was he still alive?

Feet thudded closer. Egil looked up. "Heimdal, protect me!" he whispered.

The Heir in Harlan stood over him, stunner at ready. Harlan grunted. "Not dead. Good. It was hard to guess how much power to use on someone your size." He holstered the stunner. "I have no quarrel with you, off-worlder, so I haven't killed you, but I can't have you on my tail. Go back where you belong. Let the new Lharr in Halarek learn by himself the lesson about Harlan his sire and grandsire learned."

Harlan bent and searched Egil expertly. He took the stunner and its spare power pack, some food, and the map. He unfolded the map. His eyes followed the line and he nodded. "That was a tough man, Halarek's serf-soldier. I should've guessed he'd do something like this." Harlan stuffed the map into an inside pocket of his parka. "Go home. I'll kill you if I see you after me again. I'll kill Halarek for sure. Later. Right now I have troubles of my own." Harlan checked the power level of his stunner, pointed it at Egil, and fired. Egil knew nothing more.

He awoke in the dark of mountain night. Stars sparkled sharp and clear like ice chips above him. Now and then Tarval's wrinkled blue face peeked down through the gently waving tops of the trees. Egil tried to raise his arm, but the arm would not obey him. He lay still, cursing silently and then out loud. Despite Egil's care, Harlan had sneaked up on him. Now the man was escaping and it might be yet more hours before Egil could start after him. Thinking of the hours ahead of him, wakeful but inactive, made Egil crawl inside.

He would not waste the time until he could move again. He would check on Harlan, then Karne. During the chase, he had concentrated on Harlan of necessity. Now he had time, lots of time, though he wished he did not. Egil, with difficulty, cleared the chase and Harlan from his mind and went into the necessary receptive state for Seeing. His time for Harlan was very short. Harlan was continuing toward the pass into the steppes beyond Konnor Holding. Egil then visualized Karne and also the sun at midday, the time when Karne and his house officers usually worked on manor business.

Tane Orkonan sat at the library worktable, bent over correspondence. Weisman was digging in a cabinet toward the back of the room, sneezing periodically from the dust he was stirring up. Karne stood beside the fireplace looking down into the flames, a letter hanging from his hand. He was talking to Tane.

"—thin and bony and sick. Lizanne was all I could get from the Houses as a wife! The sick, the infertile, the ugly, that's all I was offered. Girls only the desperate would take. Thin and bony and sick she is. Is she infertile, too?" Karne's hand shook so the letter in it rattled. "And her sire wants an entire *holding* as bride price, though she may be as barren as her sister." Karne slammed his fist into the surface of the fireplace; it looked more like a gesture of despair than of anger. "Damn them all to hell! House Halarek needs heirs! Does everyone still see the end of this House at Harlan hands, even when Richard Harlan's in *prison*?"

Orkonan looked up from his work. He sighed heavily. "Your sire did you no benefit, Karne. It may take years to prove how wrong he was about you."

"And in the meantime?"

"In the meantime, you do the best you know how. Are you asking my advice about this letter from House Arnette?"

"I guess so. Who else *can* I ask? Brinnd has gone. Weisman has never been more than a clerk. Emil von Schuss—perhaps I could talk to Emil, but it would have to be a personal visit."

"Trouble with people tapping into the tri-d signal again?"

Karne sighed and nodded. "Will I ever get used to living this way? I was used to it once. I must have been, but now I miss Balder so much!"

Orkonan looked at Karne very seriously. His face worked briefly, as if what he was about to say was difficult for him. "You did your duty to your House and Family, lord. I'll always admire you for that. The temptation not to must have been almost overwhelming."

Karne flushed slightly. "Thanks, Tane. That means a lot to me." His voice was husky.

Orkonan looked down at the tabletop and shuffled papers around noisily for a moment. "About Lizanne Arnette . . . "

"What do you think?"

"What do *you* think?"

"I think she's the last of a sickly line. Worse, the line produces very few girls. Very few."

"Is that an issue here, Karne?"

Karne just looked at him.

"Okay, okay. Girls. Alliances. Prestige. A visible sign to the—the—I can't think of a fitting word. A sign to some that the Four Guardians hold you in the palms of their hands. House Harlan has made a great many alliances on the girls it's bred." Tane looked thoughtful. "Could you find a wife at Harlan's source?"

Karne's mouth twisted into a bitter smile. "Where would this House find the money to refurbish one of the Council's ships? If Harlan alliances in Council didn't prevent leasing one in the first place."

"You could at least try, Karne. The mortgages from the Farm 3 business are almost paid off. Perhaps—you could try, lord."

Karne's mouth twisted even more. "Which humiliation would be worse for my House: being turned down by Council or taking someone like Lizanne Arnette to wife?"

• • •

Egil fell asleep, as sometimes happened during a Seeing. When he awoke, the forest gleamed green and gold in late-afternoon sunlight. He sat up slowly. Everything worked again. He clenched and unclenched his hands, just to be sure. He looked around. Here, almost at ground level, Egil saw hardy wildflowers, blooming in the brief, brief warmth of summer in the Frozen Zone. Some tiny animal scurried under the needles nearby, making the fallen pine needles rustle and quiver. A shrew or vole or Starker IV's equivalent, Egil told himself. He dug through the pack. Harlan appeared to have taken only what Egil had seen him take.

Egil stood, brushed dry needles from himself, and started off downslope. Harlan had been heading steadily toward the pass into the steppes beyond House Konnor. Egil would act as if that was what Harlan would continue to do until a Seeing or a sighting told him otherwise. Egil acknowledged with some bitterness that a sighting would be most unlikely, considering Harlan had almost a day's start. Through a moment's carelessness, he had lost Harlan and his own freedom. Even if he caught up again, what could he do with no weapon but the axe, which only killed? It was just a matter of time before the Watchers Saw what had happened and snatched him back.

As he trudged downhill, Egil went over and over the minutes before Harlan shot him. He could see nothing more he could have done. If he had just circled that clump of trees first, he would have seen there was no trail on the downslope side. Or maybe Harlan *had* laid one. Or maybe . . . For hours as he walked he went over and over the last day. He did not know what he could have done differently.

Shortly after sunrise the next morning, Egil sat concealed at the foot of a cliff on the south side of the pass. He had heard fliers passing over in the night. One had flown close enough over his campsite that it might have spotted the glow from his thermo, if that was the sort of thing it was looking for. And it had definitely been looking for something. It had been circling and, although its circles had finally taken it out of hearing, there was no reason to take chances. The flier could be anyone's. He was afraid it was Harlan's. Who else would search in the Frozen Zone? Who else knew there was anyone there?

The morning air was chilly and damp from an earlier mist; the grass and stones were wet with mist and dew. Eastward, a piece of the cliff had fallen sometime in the past, littering the ground with chunks and blocks of rock in many sizes. A flow of gravel and small rocks filled many of the gaps between the fallen blocks and chunks and flowed on out beyond the jumble to form a delta perhaps 250 meters wide. Beyond that was the lower slope of this mountain, and a smaller mountain, and the foothills beyond that and then the steppes of Konnor and Neeran and York spreading yellow-green and beige-brown across the background.

Egil got up and walked out of the cliff's shadow to examine the slopes below and the foothills beyond. On the vast grasslands of the foothills, herds grazed, black and brown specks on the yellow-green background. How did Harlan plan to get across the open without detection? Disguise himself as a herdsman? Somehow Egil could not see the Heir in Harlan lowering himself so far as to dress like a serf, even to save his own life.

Egil sighed. He could do another Seeing, but unless he recognized the landscape, Seeing where Harlan was at the moment would not help find him. The last time he had used the Seeing for location, the god had provided Anse-the-smith. Since the ford, Egil's luck had gone. The god's favor was gone, and there was no deciphering what had happened. Egil stood, looked across the wilderness of rock and trees, and felt a terrible despair. How was he ever to find Harlan again in this? Was he to be imprisoned forever underground for one stupid mistake? Were his dreams of earning a place in his family forever smashed?

A small voice inside scolded him. "You *have* a solid place in your family. You are as loved and liked as any of the others. Whether you're famous or not doesn't matter to them."

"But it matters to *me*," Egil whispered.

He sighed again and started across the slope. To be with the Watchers forever. To lose all chances for fame or wealth or glory—

Egil heard a flier's engine. It was coming back. Egil spun and dashed for the shelter of the large rock. Gravel sank beneath his toes and sprayed out behind him as he ran. He ducked under the cliff just in time, for the flier passed right overhead. Its engine noise reverberated from the cliff. Its broad shadow sailed past, and then the ship itself came into view as it crossed downslope, a small, red, four-man flitter. It disappeared again as it circled above the cliff, but it did not go away. Its engines thrummed, loud in the vast stillness.

The flier was definitely looking for something. Or someone. It circled again. Lower. Closer.

At least its sender isn't trying to conceal it, painted red like it is, Egil thought. So it isn't likely a friend of Harlan's. On the other hand, I've learned how daring Richard Harlan is. Maybe he *would* use a red flier.

CHAPTER 13

Egil slid the pack from his back and flattened himself against the rock as best he could. The flier came past in an even tighter circle, banked, swooped low over Egil's back trail. Egil's heart stopped. The gravel! He had run through gravel and that marked his location as well as a signpost would. Egil pulled his axe free of its straps. It wasn't much of a weapon against the weapons of this world, but it was better than nothing, and only Harlan's people knew anyone was in the Frozen Zone.

The red flier set down somewhere nearby with the sizzle and hiss of hot metal on wet grass, then Egil heard two or more pairs of feet crunching over the gravel. His mouth felt dry. He braced himself and waited for the newcomers to make the first move.

"You there!" The voice was strained.

Egil loosened his shoulders and lifted the axe.

"We're Council men," the voice shouted. "Don't shoot."

Shoot? Egil's mouth quirked. *Obviously they don't know my last encounter with Harlan lost me the stunner. So they're not Harlan supporters or at least haven't talked to him recently.*

Something stirred in the back of Egil's mind. Council men. Council men wore red. Because of the Freemen and minor Houses, Council now stood neutral in fact in Karne's feud, as it had always stood neutral in theory. Egil let himself relax a little. At least he was not going to be shot down on sight.

The same voice called the same message in the pidgin the Runners sometimes used. That gave Egil another clue: They didn't know whom they had cornered.

Egil hesitated another moment, weighing what he knew about Council and Gharr politics against the other possible dangers, then stepped into the open and waited, hands held well away from his sides. That was not a good position from which to effectively use an axe, as even these men, who had never used such a weapon, must see.

Three men in Council red came round the end of the cliff. They fanned out and came toward Egil cautiously, hands near their weapons. When they were close enough to see his face clearly, they stopped abruptly and stared at him. Egil flexed his hands, feeling suddenly nervous. *What's the matter with them? Haven't they ever seen an off-worlder before?*

The man in the lead stepped a pace forward. His right hand now rested on the handle of his stunner. His fingers flipped open the weapon's retainer strap.

"Identify yourself." The man's voice had a slight tremor in it and he seemed pale, though it was hard to tell when the Gharr were pale.

Egil stiffened. "Why do you ask? I'm not the one with weapon at ready. I've bothered no one and there are no rules against traveling here, are there?"

The speaker cleared his throat. "We—ah—we don't mean to offend. Ah—what is considered courtesy on your world?"

"Hands away from weapons, for one."

"That's not what I meant. You are not a lord, so you can't be called 'my lord' and . . . "

"I'm called Egil Olafsson, gentlehom."

" 'Gentlehom' is what I meant, gentlehom." The man cleared his throat again and his finger and thumb rubbed the loosened retainer strap. "We don't mean to offend, but no one ever travels up here. No"—he raised his hand deprecatingly—"it's not that it's illegal, it's that no one

can live here long. We're here only because Gild pix—
from their orbiter, gentlehom; I'm sure you must know of
it—Gild pix showed tracks in the snow farther up. There
shouldn't be tracks there. And once there was a figure
in the geyser basin that wasn't a Zinn bear. We had to
investigate, gentlehom. It's our duty. A convicted murderer
recently escaped from Breven and . . . " He looked down a
moment. "We saw the tracks above on the tundra and then
some down here and thought they might be his, you see."
He met Egil's eyes. "No one could've imagined they'd
be yours. You've been dead—believed dead—for nearly
a year."

Egil let out a long breath and allowed his hands to drop
to his sides. He thought about Harlan with increasing hope.
He had not come down to the steppes, after all. He had kept
to the tundra above the tree line, where the footing was poor
and visibility high and where energy was spent faster than at
lower altitudes. He would have to come out of the Frozen
Zone soon. The fact that he took food proved that.

Perhaps I have a chance to catch him after all, Egil
thought. *But first I have to get rid of the Council men.*

Egil thought of his vow to tell no one where he'd been
or what had happened to him during his time away. Now
that he faced the first questioners, he suddenly realized how
very, very hard that vow would be to keep. He could dream
up something to explain everything except the healing of
his hands, even how he came to have survived in the
Frozen Zone. But his hands—such freezing did not mend.
The hands had been doomed. Now they functioned. Self-
consciously he clasped them behind his back. The Council
men shifted their feet, waiting for an explanation, probably.
Well, there wasn't one, not one he could give without
breaking at least one vow.

He looked over his shoulder at the pass. Almost a day.
Harlan had almost a day's lead. But he hadn't crossed the
pass, according to what the Council men had seen. He was
planning to come out of the Zone some other way, then.
Maybe these men know where. It was time to set a trap
for Harlan. It would be Egil's last chance to catch Harlan

before he reached whatever protection he was after. Only Harlan was still free and Egil had been found. The Halareks, Council, even his family would know he was still alive and if anyone figured out he was after Harlan, Council would take over the hunt. It was Council's laws he had broken. *Well, Council can't have him.*

Council can't have him. Egil rubbed his right palm back and forth across his left hand. *I'll have to be very lucky to get out of this and the god has withheld his help and his luck lately. Is the god still watching?*

The leader of the Council soldiers was speaking to Egil. "Gentlehom, Lord Karne offered a very large reward for your safe return, and a large reward just for news of what happened to you." The man left a hopeful silence, waiting for Egil to fill it.

He would have to. Egil cast about quickly for something safe to say. He looked the leader in the eye, trying to create an impression of earnestness and of the importance of his words, one of the Academy's techniques. "Tell Lord Karne that I'm healthy and safe and that his business is progressing as well as can be expected. I'll be at Halarek in another week, perhaps two." He altered his expression to one he hoped looked apologetic and wished he had paid as much attention during the classes in "diplomatic presentation" as Karne had. Karne had gotten very good about wrapping a role around himself and convincing his audience he was confident or appreciative or whatever. "I've had no way to reach him and I'm not yet finished."

"Business? In the Frozen Zone?" The man's tone implied the idea was absolutely unbelievable.

Egil was afraid. He saw his freedom disappearing permanently. "Yes. Business." His voice was icy and shook a little. He turned to pick up his pack.

"Stop." The leader took an impulsive step forward, looked at the axe, and stopped. "You can't leave. The Lharr Halarek looked for you for more than four months, until Uhl stopped him, as a matter of fact."

Egil did not look around, hoping that would help hide the tremor in his voice. "I can appreciate the gesture and still leave to finish my work." He hoisted the pack onto his shoulders.

"What business?" The man's voice was suddenly very suspicious.

Egil wondered if he dared just walk away. He took a step and saw from the corner of his eye the soldiers' taut faces and the fingers hovering over stunners. They had seen a ghost, or what should have been a ghost, and in an area of the world where no one went, at least as far as the noble Houses and the Freemen knew. They were frightened. To walk back into the unknown world of the Frozen Zone would push them past what they would believe. He was alive, yes. That he was on secret business for a lord, probably. That he had business where nothing was, no. If he wanted to finish his hunt, he could not just walk away. He turned back carefully.

"I'm the Lharr's brother-by-rite. That means I do as he asks, even as his soldiers do." It was not the truth, exactly, but it was a philosophy they could understand. But they still looked suspicious and their hands still hovered near their weapons. "Look, all the lords of the Gharr have secret business, even the Lharr Halarek. Every minute I spend arguing with you makes my job more and more impossible, and if you keep me standing here much longer, I'll lose what chance I had to complete it. I'll be disgraced." That, too, he hoped they would understand.

The leader looked doubtful. "It's true we *don't* have orders to bring *you* in."

One of the other men stepped quickly to his side and whispered urgently into his ear. Egil saw the leader's hand move and a moment later he was facedown in the snow, unable to move. Fury burned through him. Harlan would escape. Karne would go under. All because some middle-class military bureaucrats—

The men bound his hands quickly, then turned him over so he could breathe. The leader knelt beside him.

"Our regrets, gentlehom, but the Lharr's reward—we three can live comfortably for the rest of our lives on our shares of that reward and we're quite sure he'll pay it, even though the search's been off since Uhl. We won't keep you long, though. Three or four hours. Surely three or four hours can make no difference to work that's been under way since you disappeared."

All Egil could do was sputter helplessly. He could not even curse the men who were taking from him his chance for reputation and freedom.

The other two Council soldiers carried Egil to their flier. They propped him in one of the rear seats, belted him in, and climbed in after. The leader commed Council the moment he settled into his seat. He requested that Council ask the Lharr Halarek to meet the flier at a midpoint, the name of which Egil did not recognize.

"We're closing out Project Blue," he added.

The voice on the other end gabbled something.

"Project Blue," the leader repeated.

The voice on the other end squeaked, said something, and went away.

The leader checked out his craft, flipped switches and turned knobs, and the flier lifted off, banked over the mountain peaks, and turned southwest. A wind blew threads and streamers of snow over billowing fields of snow centuries old.

Egil sat bent backward over his bound hands, his spine in agony from the combination of snug belt and hands trapped behind, his left foot going to sleep from the weight of the pack lying on it. In his head, he consigned the men to Hel, to Hell, to the Great Abyss, to the jaws of Fenris Wolf. He squirmed to try to relieve some of the strain and only managed to get enough leverage to boot the pack off his foot.

The moment he could make his numbed mouth shape words, he grated out, "You're—destroying—weeks—of—work."

The older of the two common soldiers turned to him. "Now, you're just angry, gentlehom. Ain't nothing a three- or four-hour delay's going to hurt."

"And whatever you're doing," the leader added, "can't be as important as finding you or Lord Richard. But you probably don't know, being out of touch so long. Lord Richard has escaped."

Egil felt as if he'd explode! He could now make himself understood, if with difficulty, and he could say nothing. He wished fervently for Loki's talents at invention and fabrication, but the gods did not grant wishes. Frustration ate into him until he felt he could put a fist through a stone wall.

The opening roar that always accompanied the serving of a Halarek Family meal had died to a strong background murmur as the family and assorted guests—there were always assorted guests—settled into the serious business of eating the big meal of the day. First Day services had been shorter than usual, so the meal was early. Karne was glad, because he was very hungry.

"Milord?" A very small page tugged at Karne's sleeve. "Milord, Chairman Gashen wishes to speak to you at once."

Karne frowned at the boy, who should have had better training than to actually touch his lord in summons, glanced across Lizanne at Kathryn, then at the page, then rose swiftly from the table. Lizanne could not discipline the page. She couldn't discipline any servant. She knew too well how the blows and kicks directed at servants in most Houses felt. No, Kathryn would have to take care of whatever discipline was necessary for the page, perhaps no more than making him repeatedly practice suitable approaches to a lord. That was a simple matter. When the Chairman of Council called, it was never a simple matter. In Karne's experience, a tri-d call from the chairman meant bad news.

Karne resisted the urge to sprint to the tri-d room and get the bad news over with. Sprinting would not help, but it would give cousins and servants the idea that the Lharr in Halarek ran to a summons by a Freeman. That was not a good impression to leave with either group.

Forms, appearances, rituals, Karne grumbled to himself. *By the Guardians, I'd like to live without them for awhile!*

The com-tech waiting by the tri-d room door opened it and stepped back so Karne could enter. His boot heels clicked on the stone floor. Hareem Gashen appeared to be pacing back and forth at the far end of the Halarek tri-d room, only he paced on carpet and the rich wood paneling of the Council chairman's office gleamed behind him. That luxury was a strong contrast to Karne's own stark, technical tri-d room. Trev Halarek had seen to it that there was no "effeminate" softness here. No carpets, no padded chairs, no paneling, not even paint on the walls.

Karne bent his head toward the chairman. "Frem Gashen."

Gashen stopped his pacing and looked toward Karne. "My lord. Is your tri-d room secure? This is a shielded signal." The chairman rested his hands on his generous belly while he waited for Karne to clear his room of listeners.

Karne motioned the tri-d techs out of the room. When the last shut the door behind himself, Karne turned again to the chairman. "We are alone now, gentlehom."

The fingers of the chairman's right hand drummed lightly on the taut expanse of belly. "We—ah—we have received a most peculiar communication, my lord. Based on Gild pix, we have had patrols over the northern Frozen Zone for several days. The Gild pix showed a figure that was not a Zinn bear in a geyser basin up there, and tracks that were not characteristic of any animal we know of. So Council has been patrolling on the thought that this might be Harlan's hiding place." Gashen's mouth pursed and he looked down at his belly for a moment. "My lord, just a few minutes ago, a patrol flitter captured someone in the northern Frozen Zone—are you sure your reception is secure?"

"As secure as we can make it, Frem Gashen."

The chairman nodded. "Our men captured Egil Olafsson, my lord."

For Karne, time stopped for a moment. Egil. Found. After all this time, and in a Frozen Zone! Egil the painter. Egil the fighter. Big, blond, laughing Egil. Alive after all this time!

Then the hard-learned lessons of life among the Gharr interfered. "Who else knows?" Karne asked, rather more sharply than he intended.

"No one, I believe, unless someone has both tied into our secured signals *and* cracked today's code."

"Where is he?"

"At a safe place about four hours flight from you. We would have brought him directly to Ontar, but he insisted he was in the Frozen Zone on business and that Council's men would ruin his chances of finishing that business by taking him in." The chairman's face took on a rueful cast. "You see, my lord, the men believe they've earned the reward you promised last year at this time for Frem Olafsson's return."

Karne's mind raced. *In a Frozen Zone? Nothing lived in the Frozen Zones. Egil must have thought saying he was on my business would keep him out of Council hands, because it certainly couldn't stand up as an excuse after I show astonishment. And I did show it. Guardians! After a year! Even the Academy wouldn't expect me to look neutral after thinking him dead a year!* He smoothed his excitement and joy from his face and voice as best he could.

"Of course I'll reward them, Chairman Gashen." *Though money's quite short right now,* he added to himself. "Where is he?"

"A Council ship will take you there."

Newly relearned alarms went off inside Karne. He shook his head. "I mean no insult, Frem Gashen, but after what happened to my mother, you can understand that I don't want to trust myself to any fliers but my own."

"I'm merely attempting to keep the young man's existence as secret as possible. That seemed to be your wish, too, since you offered a reward for his return, though he was on your House's business. A very convincing cover, my lord."

Karne inclined his head in thanks. He did not think for a moment that the chairman believed Egil's story, especially after his own betraying reaction, but Gashen was accepting it, at least for now. Karne cleared his throat to remove the huskiness this kindness brought on. "You are most careful, Frem Gashen, and I'm grateful. Perhaps I could come to a meeting point and pick up a reliable Council pilot? I truly hesitate to use equipment that has not been checked by my own people."

"Understandable, my lord. You're what? Four hours from Council ground? There will be a secure pilot waiting for you there, my lord." And Gashen disappeared, without waiting for thanks or further questions.

Karne spun and dashed toward the door. Then he remembered and skidded to a stop. This had to be a secret trip, at least until he found out what had happened. He must not show his excitement. He put on a sober face and walked out the door and back to the Great Hall, though it took all the control he had. A year, and Egil was still alive! Not just alive, but well enough, whole enough, to be wandering through a Frozen Zone.

Some hours later a Council pilot brought Karne's flitter down beside a Council guardpost on the north edge of Zinn. The post was apparently not being used, since there was only one other flitter shedded there, a red four-man. Tracks made by four men led through the snow to the door of the post. No tracks came out. Karne waited only until the pilot had turned off the engines before he was out the door, skidding across the wing, sliding to the ground.

Unseemly haste, Karne told himself, but this time he did not rein in his joy. The post's door was sliding open as he reached the building. He leaped up into the space before the door was all the way open.

"Egil? Egil?"

The familiar tall, broad figure came thundering down the stairs from the turret. Egil shouted, "Karne!" and then they were on each other, laughing, hugging, pounding shoulders, shouting questions, laughing some more, fighting off the inclination to cry a little because of their powerful emotions. At last they stopped, panting and grinning like fools, and stared at each other.

"Married, eh?"

"Your hands! You're using your hands!"

"You go first," said Egil, hoping to gain a few minutes' time to think of adequate semitruthful explanations.

"No, you. And how did you know I was married?"

The Council men slipped into their parkas, Karne's pilot nodded goodbye, and they all filed out of the guardpost. The men were giving them the privacy so rare in Gharr life. And they trusted him to take care of their reward. That was a gift few Gharr lords would get. A few minutes later, the red Council flitter took off.

Egil rubbed his left hand with his right and looked down at them for a moment. "I was taken in by the local residents, so to speak." He hoped Karne would assume he meant Runners and would ask no more questions about that. It would hurt to have to lie to his best friend. And if Karne insisted on more detail, Egil would have to lie a lot. "My hands— I can't explain how they recovered. It was a miracle, as far as I'm concerned." He would willingly swear before all the gods *that* part was true. The healing *had* been a miracle. "A very, very slow miracle, Karne. They aren't back to full strength yet."

"Show me," Karne ordered, grinning. He felt so good about Egil's recovery he imagined he could float right up to the ceiling if he just took a deep breath. A friend! Among all the enemies and sometimes-allies, his *friend* was back! Back from the dead! He extended his right hand.

Egil grasped it and squeezed until Karne's knees bent.

Karne laughed. "That's not full strength? Guardians be thanked you didn't use full strength on me!" He winced then and tried to extricate his hand. "You can let go now."

Egil slapped Karne's shoulder with one hand and, a fraction of a second later, extended his other hand with the smoothness of long practice to catch his slighter friend as he staggered forward. "And you—you're a husband before you're twenty."

Karne shrugged off Egil's hand and turned away. When he spoke, his voice was low and subdued. "House Halarek must have heirs. Kit and I are all that's left. Would that I could have waited until I was twenty-five or thirty, as you can." He turned back to look at Egil. "How do you know I have a wife?"

"Oh, it was a piece of the gossip the Council men fed me on my way here." That reminded Egil of his grievance against the Council men. "Karne, I was hard on Harlan's tail when these bureaucrats knocked me out and hauled me over here. He has almost a day's lead on me through my own stupidity, but if you can guess who he's running to, I could still get him. He was headed through Konnor Holding, but—"

"Richard's going through Konnor?"

"Konnor. I've been chasing him since late Verdain over a great deal of the Frozen Zone. I've had competition from time to time. Assassins and/or cousins with assassination in mind. Council soldiers kept Harlan from running directly home. But I suppose you know that."

Karne nodded, but Egil saw from his eyes that his friend had a lot of questions that he was not going to ask at the moment. But he would ask them, eventually. Right now, Karne's primary concern was the danger a free Richard Harlan represented for Karne's house. Karne frowned and the hand he had been running through his hair stopped where it was, brown fingers interlaced with dark brown hair. He stood like that, lost in thought, for several minutes.

Karne's hand fell to his side. He looked slowly up at Egil. "He's headed for Kingsland. I'm sure of it. Lord Nellis had an unfortunate 'accident' in Koort, just before the siege, and Ingold is now earl in Kingsland. Nellis was slow, but he wasn't stupid and he was just. Ingold is Richard's ally. Ingold is Richard's sort."

Egil nodded as if listening carefully. This matched what the Watchers had said about Harlan.

Karne's eyes suddenly lit up. "I'd be willing to bet that a flitter from Kingsland will set down soon at the edge of the Frozen Zone. Near York, maybe, or even at the edge of Council ground." His voice took on a bitter edge. "That would be Richard's idea of humor, to be picked up, a fugitive from Council, at the borders of Council ground, perhaps on Council ground itself."

Egil threw his hands outward in impatience. "Look, Karne, if you think you know where he's going, every minute I spend here talking is a minute Harlan spends getting closer to safety. Especially if you're right and he's going to be picked up by a flier somewhere along the border here."

"Why didn't you tell Council where he was when you had the chance?"

Egil stared at his friend. He had expected Karne to under-stand. "*I* want Richard. I want to get him my*self*. I want to tear him limb from limb and joint from joint my*self*." Now came the hard part. "I want to, but I'm going to return him to prison. I'm betting Harlan will think that's far worse than any torture I could come up with, and I came up with some pretty good ones."

Karne went white. "You planned to let him *live*? After what he's done to my House? To Mother? After what he's done to your hands? You were going to let him *live*? I thought the Viking kind believed in *vengeance*!"

Egil looked at Karne with dismay. Not so long ago he had felt the same way. He still did, so how could he explain Harlan's necessity to Starker IV's future without bringing in the Watchers? He couldn't. He cleared his throat.

"Karne, I did intend to kill Richard myself. Then I learned how his cousins began squabbling over control of Harlan the minute after he was sentenced. If Council takes Richard back to Breven, he'll stay there the rest of his sentence and House Harlan will collapse in quarrels and family infighting. Since assassins were hunting Richard, too, you know the Harlan cousins don't intend Richard to live out his sentence. House Harlan won't survive in one piece and *that's* worse than pain or death for Richard Harlan."

Karne looked dubious. Egil knew that inside Karne the desire to do Harlan great harm fought both reason and com-mon sense. Reason and common sense told him there was no better revenge than putting Harlan back into Breven to watch his House collapse from its own greed and treachery. Richard Harlan would suffer more torment than the damned watching his weaker cousins fight over the dukedom.

Karne could not believe Egil was saying what he was hearing him say. He felt betrayed, and by the man he trusted most. He heard the reason and common sense in Egil's words, but reason and common sense could not disarm his rage. Harlan *dared* to kill the Larga. He *dared* to aim for Kit.

Karne shook his head as if to rid it of those thoughts. To wonder at Richard's actions was to think as if he were still on Balder. For most of Gharr history, a woman expected to become the property of the man who killed her father, brother, husband, or other protector. Such forced "wooing" would be accepted even now, should Richard succeed in defeating Halarek. Anger flooded Karne.

Not my sister! I'll kill her myself before he puts a hand on her. I'll kill him first.

The Academy-trained part of Karne watched, amazed and helpless, as months of suppressed anger and humiliation swamped the practicalities of allowing the natural order of Gharr politics to take care of Richard Harlan. The Gharr-raised side of Karne took over. Karne heard himself rationalizing a violent death for the duke-designate and was helpless to turn the process off.

A Lharr's most important duty was to keep his House safe, the Gharr-raised Karne argued, and giving Richard the death he so thoroughly deserved would be a giant step toward that safety. Karne's new vassals were settling in, Ontar and the Holding were recovering from the strain of defending against two sieges in one year, and he had the bride his House needed.

"I'm going along." The words were out of his mouth and they felt right. The Academy's diplomat/peace negotiator was horrified.

Egil's mouth fell open. "No. You aren't prepared. You have no supplies. Your House—"

Karne was already opening cabinet doors. The guardposts in Zinn always had a stock of food, arms, bedding, medical equipment. Egil could be persuaded to change his mind while Karne collected what he would need. "There are supplies here. I'll be ready in five minutes. Nik has been managing the Holding while I was out fighting. He can keep on doing so." Mentally Karne added, *And Lady Agnes will keep him and Kit as separate as if he were at home on von Schuss Holding. Guardians! I wish our House could afford such a marriage, but we are already closely allied. Kit must marry elsewhere.*

"I'm not going anywhere, Karne, until I'm sure Harlan will be as safe in your hands as I am."

Egil's quiet voice cut Karne's thoughts into untidy pieces. Karne looked at his friend in amazement. "After what Richard's done?"

"After what he's done. I've—I've sworn to my rescuers to return him to Breven safely. I took an oath, Karne, an oath in their temple."

Karne studied Egil in silence. He knew how much the keeping of oaths meant to him. He also sensed there was much Egil was not telling him. Richard deserved to die. Halarek deserved that protection. But without Egil's cooperation, there would be no capture: Egil knew approximately where Richard was. If Karne was to have any chance at all of catching Richard, even if that meant returning him to Council hands, he would have to promise Egil not to kill Richard. It was that simple in the end. No promise equaled no Richard. Egil was not going to budge on this one.

Karne sighed heavily. This decision would cost his House, but not as much as allowing Richard to meet his allies would cost it. "Egil, I swear by my mother's blood that I won't damage Richard."

CHAPTER 14

In what seemed to Egil no time at all, Karne had collected survival gear and the two of them were climbing onto the wing of the remaining flitter and into its cabin. Karne piloted by unspoken agreement: He knew the territory outside the Zone, at least marginally. Karne lifted the flitter abruptly out of the guardpost's clearing and flew it east toward Konnor and Council ground.

"Lacked a little finesse," Egil commented mildly.

"That's what Nik always says." Karne adjusted a few knobs, set a switch, and leaned back in his seat. "No more work for a half hour or so, until we're over Konnor Holding. Tane's Family," he added for Egil's benefit. "Vassals of mine. I don't expect they'd give Richard any help. I wish I could say that of all of them. Tell me what's been going on."

Egil summarized what had happened, leaving out the serf-villagers and the Watchers. He could tell from Karne's face that his friend knew he was leaving a lot out. Egil attempted to divert his attention. "Do you suspect *your* vassals may be helping Harlan?"

Karne's face was grim. "Perhaps. Roul holds no love for me. And Nerut. And Melevan. And some or all of the holdings I won from Harlan. Roul, Nerut, and Melevan think they have a grievance because I defeated them without 'fighting like a man.' In *Uhl* they wanted me to fight! Or maybe they thought I'd wait to deal with them until fighting weather in the spring." Karne snorted. "I may still be naive about politics and possibilities on this world, Egil, but I'm not *stupid*!"

Egil looked out of the side window so Karne could not read his thoughts from his face. *That's what stings, isn't it, my friend? That the Academy's brilliant negotiator gets shown up too often here because he has the wrong skills.*

They cast about for hours, but saw neither trace of Harlan on the ground nor of Harlan or Odonnel fliers in the sky. They did see three Council fliers in that time, however. Egil presumed they were looking for the escapee. Karne had perhaps come to the same conclusion. His movements became more and more abrupt, his sentences shorter, his tone curter. Impatience shouted from every line of his body. Egil had the feeling that, if he were the pilot, he'd be reacting to the frustration in much the same way. It was maddening to know your enemy was within reach and be unable to find him or to call for help from home. Any com signal would give their location to Harlan and Council both and right now Karne wanted Harlan outside Council protection as much as Egil did.

Flying was the only possible way to find Harlan first. Looking on foot would take far too much time, even if they could find any traces of Harlan's passing, which Egil doubted. The man would've covered his tracks. Egil felt as sure as Karne did that time was running out. Rescue had to be just around the corner for Harlan.

Egil glanced at Karne. Karne was preoccupied with his piloting and his frustrated searching. Maybe he could get by with a Seeing while Karne was thinking about other things. A Seeing had found Harlan before. Egil leaned back in his seat, made himself breathe slowly and evenly, and imagined Harlan's face. Now. He wanted to See Harlan now.

It was some time before anything but the blur of the flitter cabin filled Egil's eyes. Then he was on a mountain slope looking down on a wide, shallow river moving through even wider kilometers of marsh. It was early morning and, even in summer, early mornings in the Frozen Zone left a lacy edging of ice along the shallows of the river. Egil squinted his eyes against the sun. The river ran south and wound through mountains. Upstream, the glittering ribbon of river passed through a gap in the mountains, and beyond that gap, steam rose across the horizon. Richard Harlan stood on a large flat rock in the middle of the river, waving and motioning.

Egil sat bolt upright. "Karne!"

Karne stiffened and his hand was on the flitter's firing buttons instantly.

"Hey, Karne, I'm sorry. I should know better than to shout like that."

Karne lifted his hand from the firing controls. "At least *that* instinct works as it should." His voice was bitter and self-judging. He reset the autopilot, looked at Egil, and waited.

"If I can describe where Harlan was this morning, can you find it?"

Karne gave Egil a puzzled look, but nodded.

Egil described the river he had Seen. Karne called up the map function on the flitter's navigational screen and diddled with the controls. The words on the screen meant nothing to Egil—he could speak Rom but had never learned to read it—but the landscape looked promising. "There," he said, pointing to a place on a river which came from the geyser basin and wound between mountains.

Karne called up closer detail. The screen showed a wide sickly-green space on this river. The color meant wet, low land. Egil pointed to it. "Can we try there?"

Karne gave him the same puzzled look, but took the flitter off automatic, changed the controls, reset automatic, and sat back in his seat. He folded his arms across his chest and stared at Egil. "And?"

Egil bristled defensively. "If he's not there, what have we lost?"

"Nothing. I'm just curious how you come to know of this marshy place in a part of *my* world that even *my* people don't visit. Have you been studying Gild pix while you were in hiding? That's something we haven't gotten to yet. Where you've been all this time and what you've been doing and *why you didn't let your friends know you were still alive!*"

Egil swallowed. "I couldn't and I can't. Not yet. I've sworn oaths not to, Karne. And I had no way to reach you. How could the Runners com Halarek, even if they'd wanted to? I've been a *prisoner*, Karne!" Karne's suspicion hurt.

"A prisoner. And they just let you go. Just like that. After they'd healed your hands."

Egil heard the hardening of Karne's voice. He could understand his skepticism, even suspicion, but understanding did not make the hurt less. "Karne! Damn it to all Hel! This is me, Egil, you're talking to. Not Harlan. Not Odonnel. Not even one of your stinking, slinking vassals. It's *me*! We've been friends for years."

Karne's voice was lower now and dangerously calm. His right hand held a stunner Egil had not even seen him draw. "I thought we were friends, too. But hands that were frozen into blocks don't work like new again. Ever. I've been trying to figure out who you are and who's paying you and why, but I can't. Assassination? Kidnapping? Kit? Richard wants Kit. Does someone else? Do you work for Richard? Are you an android? Who are you really and how did you get to know so much about Egil Olafsson?"

Egil swallowed. He stared at the round brown hole at the end of the stunner's barrel. If he read the stunner's lights correctly, Karne had set the power level to "kill." Karne was serious. Egil's mind raced. Obviously he hadn't considered how his long, silent absence would look to someone whose life depended on suspicion and extreme caution. He had known that missing year would be a problem to explain, considering all he must in honor not say, but it had never occurred to him that Karne, Karne, by all the gods! would think him an imposter, an assassin, even. While he had been with the Watchers a year, Karne had lived a year with the treachery and routine betrayals of the Gharr and that had changed him. A lot. The old Karne would have suspected a plot against him or his Family—that was a given on this world—but he would not have suspected Egil.

Actually he's not suspecting me, Egil told himself. *Because my hands work now, he's suspecting I'm a synthetic, an android, and he had to react so fast to protect himself that it hasn't occurred to him that only someone with off-world experience would even be able to think of such a thing as a synthetic. The Families feel leaving the planet is disloyal, maybe traitorous. With my luck lately, though, Harlan will be one of those who's been off-world.*

Egil's racing mind brought him back to the unwavering stunner barrel and the implacable face of his friend. A glance out the windshield told him only seconds had passed. To die at Karne's hands—. Egil weighed the odds of successfully knocking the stunner out of Karne's hand before he could shoot and decided the odds were not good.

"I'm waiting for that explanation." Karne's voice was deadly.

Egil knew he'd have to come up with a very convincing explanation and there wasn't one. He knew he should have felt afraid, but what he felt was a bitter anger that years of being as close as a brother to this man had been forgotten in the bone-deep distrust that kept lords of the Gharr alive.

Karne always was a quick study, Egil thought bitterly. He wanted to slam his fist into something, but he knew any sudden motion would be his last. He let words explode instead. "Heimdal, Karne! I can't prove who I am. I'm the only one of me there is. I couldn't be an imposter. There isn't one among the Gharr big enough to be me. I haven't been here long enough for someone to custom-design a synthetic to look like me. Who on Starker IV besides you and me even knows synthetics exist? Come on! Don't expect *me* to break oaths because *your* world functions on lies and betrayal!"

That stung. Egil could see from Karne's face that that stung, but Karne's voice still came out cold, cold, cold. "Oaths to whom, Egil? Whose oath is more important than our blood oath? *Whose?*"

Egil took a deep breath. "People who hold my life and freedom, and yours, in their hands." He held up a palm to ward off questions. "They're not of this planet, if that helps any, and they're no threat to your House."

There was a com-challenge from House Konnor just then. Karne answered briefly without either taking his eyes from Egil or relaxing the position of the stunner. He took a very quick look at where they were, then continued his questions.

"My brother Egil had next to no knowledge of Starker's geography. How can you describe a place that Egil has never seen? And why do you tell me Richard will be at this place, if not to lay a trap? As I told you earlier, I'm not stupid."

Egil sighed and shook his head. He held up his right wrist with the livid scar of blood brotherhood across it. "Other than this, I have no proof of who I am, not for someone who's known me since we were cleven. I've made oaths to my healers, oaths I won't break even for you, Karne Halarek, even if you kill me for it." Egil took a deep breath and was quiet for a moment. "As for knowing where Richard of Harlan will soon be . . . " Egil sighed again and looked out the window. "I See where Harlan is, Karne, as Mother Sees. You know Mother and Solveig are sybils. Well, recently I've become one, too. Against my will, for the most part. It isn't a man's gift." Egil looked back at his friend. "But man's gift or no, I See true, and if you can find this place, you'll find Harlan. You can prove to yourself that I'm telling you the truth by going to look. Either you trust Egil Olafsson or you don't." Egil looked out the window again. "It's a sorry world where people have no one they can trust." Egil turned his back on Karne and the stunner.

There was a long silence behind him. Karne moved. Egil heard the rustle of clothing and a thud as the stunner was laid on its shelf, then Karne's hand closed on Egil's shoulder hard enough to make his bones ache. The mountains of the Zone rushed by on the left, the steppes of Gild land and Neeran below and on the right. Karne sat down again. When Egil turned, Karne was sitting hunched over, his head in his hands.

"It's the Ouse, Egil," Karne said finally, his voice almost a whisper. "The river you Saw is the Ouse. It runs past the freecity of York." He took a deep, shuddering breath. "I do remember your mother and her Gift, Egil. I remember she told me they all would die, my brothers and my sire, and I didn't believe her." Karne's voice faded away and again the cabin was silent.

Suddenly Karne's fist slammed the padded arm of his seat. "What kind of a man have I become that I threaten one of the few people I trust completely?" He stared out the windshield without seeing.

"A man whose world is too treacherous for friendship," Egil said quietly.

A little more than an hour later, the York appeared on the horizon, or rather its satellite dishes and emergency exit shelters did. Nearer, but still eastward, an oval shadow slid across the ground. Egil leaned forward to see better. A flier. It had to be a flier. The vehicle itself was concealed under a cloud. "Karne, is this thing armed?"

Karne's head snapped around. "Sort of. Why?"

Egil pointed. The flier had slipped out from under the cloud. It was purple.

"Kingsland," Karne breathed. "I was right." He leaned forward, adjusted controls, and lifted the flitter above the fluffy clouds. "Maybe we can hide, some, until we get closer."

Egil had his doubts, but he said nothing. Perhaps Karne meant only that he could hide his House colors, which meant flying higher so the purple flitter could see only the dirty, pitted underside that looked like every flitter's underside.

For a time, they gained on the Kingsland flier, then it apparently spotted them and accelerated. After that it was all Karne could do to keep the more powerful Kingsland flier in sight. The flier turned abruptly and stood out for a moment in brilliant purple against the gray rock of the mountains, then it disappeared up a valley into the Zone.

"Evasion?" Egil asked.

"Don't think so. Don't imagine the pilot thinks he needs to evade us. Look how he left us in the dust. I don't think he could see my colors, but he could certainly tell this flitter isn't Council red. No, he's looking for Richard. Hold on."

Karne jerked the flitter into a steep turn and followed the Kingsland flitter's path up the valley. "Keeps out of Council sensors, flying this low."

Karne managed to keep the craft ahead in sight, slowed as it was by bends and by sharp changes in elevations of the valley, but barely. The purple flier rose over a ridge and flew east. Karne called a ground diagram up on a control-panel screen and studied the lay of the mountains. "Looks like there's a basin or wide valley near the Ouse a little west of here," he muttered. "Bet that's where he's headed. We'll shortcut and catch him. Thank the Guardians for Gild satellite pix."

"That's how Council found me. Satellite pix."

Egil hoped his remark would draw some questions, but Karne only half heard and he continued talking, more to himself than to Egil.

"Wonder how the pilot knows where to find him. No comming. Council would hear it. Prior arrangement. Has to be. And that means at least one person in Breven helped him. I knew that, anyway. No way he could've survived here otherwise. Someone left supplies in a prearranged place. Who? House full of deacons and no way to know which one. Or ones. I can't check and Council apparently hasn't. He's almost to safety. If that flitter gets out of here, he's home, 'cause this flitter can't catch that one. Ten years younger and probably heavily armed. It would be if I were in Richard's place."

The soliloquy was getting on Egil's nerves. This driving single-mindedness was not like Karne at all. Egil cut into the flood of spoken thoughts. "When Harlan jumped me, he took my stunner and some food. He didn't kill me. Obviously."

Karne came out of his preoccupation abruptly. "Richard had you and he didn't kill you?"

Egil nodded. "He said he had no quarrel with me, told me to go home and leave you to him. Then he used my own stunner on me so he could get enough lead to lose me."

The flitter shot over the ridge. Beyond another, lower ridge was a glittering bend in a river.

"The Ouse," Karne said.

Karne slowed the flitter, but they still sailed over the next ridge at high speed. Egil kept close watch out the window. Karne would have enough to do piloting, what with tricky winds and a much higher ridge on the east side of the river. Suddenly they were across the ridge and the river was visible again. The Kingsland flier was settling on a sandbar below.

"Purple flitter, military grade, landing. Six to eight men waiting, one in Harlan green," Egil said.

Karne nodded, eyes intent on his instruments. The flitter sped over the river and the ridge beyond.

Egil stiffened and looked at Karne. "That was Harlan," he snapped. "That was *Harlan* and you flew right on by!" Egil saw his oath being swept away and his freedom with it. It was all he could do to resist ripping Karne out of the pilot's chair and taking over the controls himself.

Karne's voice and posture were stiff. "Two of us, more of them. Military flier versus Halarek-marked four-man flitter. There'd be no contest, Egil." Karne leaned forward to take a closer instrument reading, then swung the flitter southward.

"No! By all the gods, you're not quitting, Karne! I *have* to get Harlan." Egil lurched out of his seat and reached for the stick.

Karne backhanded Egil into his seat. Egil sat stunned. When Karne had reached forward that last time, he must have picked up something heavy. Egil rubbed his cheek and jaw.

Heimdal, that hurts! He looked at Karne in amazement. *I'm half again his weight. Gods, he must be angry! He's shaking, he's so angry.*

"Now who's not paying attention to what he knows?" Karne was snarling. "I have to take insults about my courage every day from enemies and Family, even though what I'm doing works better than the old ways, but by the Guardians I'll not take the same insults from you! You *know* better!"

Karne sat watching the instruments and breathing hard. Egil stared at him and at the landscape streaming by. He had done essentially the same thing Karne had, made assumptions that years of experience of what Karne was like should have told him were wrong. "Karne, I'm sorry—"

Karne jerked the flitter up and over another ridge. Egil told himself that the uneasiness in his stomach was not lack of trust in Karne's piloting, but knowing his friend, for the first time in a long time, was letting his emotions loose. Past experience told Egil that loosening caused a certain recklessness that was often hard on people nearby.

Suddenly, to the east, a flash of red dropped out of the clouds, then another. Egil pointed. "They're coming!"

Karne had already seen. He made the flitter bank suddenly and dive into a deep-cut valley. In moments, the flitter was deep among the valleys and walls, out of all possibility of Council sighting or sensing, banking, diving, skimming across almost vertical surfaces, following the contours.

"If Richard must live, Council will take him from *my* hands," Karne said fiercely. "No one else's."

The flitter's shadow skimmed along beside it, making the craft seem even closer to the granite than it was and it was very close, closer than Egil, daredevil pilot though he was, would ever have taken anything less than a stunt-flier. A gray wall rose suddenly ahead of them. Karne jerked the flitter up. Egil imagined he heard the scrape of granite across the flitter's belly. The little flier skimmed over the boulder field on top of the wall and plunged into the depths of a narrow valley. The flitter's wingtips missed the walls on either side by centimeters. Karne turned the little craft on its side around a sharp corner into a larger valley. Egil saw river water suddenly an arm's length away, foam where the river met rock, fish in a clear pool. Karne wrenched the flitter level almost at wave-tops, then they were between narrow walls again, spray glittering on the flitter's nose.

A jutting section of wall made the passage still narrower. Karne banked the flitter sharply to pass it, close enough to see the grain of the sandstone. A dark beak reared out of the shadows just ahead. The flitter banked hard right, flattened out. A sudden bend in the wall and Karne banked the flitter sharply the other way. Water riffled with the wind of their passage. The river flowed into a larger one. Sunlight. Rapids. Spray—

They were out over Harlan again before Egil realized what was happening. Karne's left hand darted under the instruments. There was a loud report from under the flitter and then a purple line traced the projectile Karne fired right to the Kingsland flitter. A second later, there was a small explosion and a cloud of smoke on one of the flitter's wings.

"Evens the odds some." Karne's face was grim. "He'd get away in that before we could take out his guards and capture him otherwise. Now *we* have a chance to get him!"

Karne rounded a bend in the river and dropped the flitter with stomach-lurching suddenness onto a damp sandbar. He sat stone-still for a long moment. Egil let himself go limp and shut his eyes.

By all the gods! And I thought I *was a pilot!* He swallowed with difficulty; his mouth was as dry as day-old toast, and as scratchy. He swallowed again and opened his eyes.

Karne twisted in his seat, made an impatient sound, unclasped his safety harness, twisted around far enough to unhook a weapons belt from a rack behind his seat. "Ouse just ahead. Grab what equipment you want. We walk from here. *This* time we'll make *sure* Council won't let the abbot be so lenient with the Harlan Heir. He'll stay in solitary if I—"

"You're *not* going to kill him?" Egil could not believe what he had heard. "Now, when you have the best chance you'll get for *years*, you're not going to kill him?"

"You swore to keep him safe. I promised you I wouldn't kill him. He's safe. This time."

The implacability in Karne's voice chilled Egil. This was not the old Karne, either. "I want Harlan to die, too, Karne, but this is by far the better revenge. Every day of his nine years at Breven he'll know his cousins and his vassals are taking his Holding apart. Long before he gets out, there'll be only crumbs left. I want him to know what's going to happen. I want him to be helpless to stop it."

Karne stared at Egil, his eyes dark and unreadable. As Egil watched, a little of Karne's tension eased out of him. He smiled a tiny, grim smile. "Richard will pray for an assassin in Breven and I'll see that security around him is so tight no assassin can get near him."

Egil knew the calm, level tone was a form, an Academy technique for expert negotiators Karne had learned far too well: "A naval pacification officer does not exhibit his feeling about an issue; he uses them, under appropriate intellectual control, to fuel effective action." Only with Karne it had often become more than a form, a mask over feelings. It had become a lid over feelings unacceptable in public. Unfortunately, on Starker IV, almost every place a Gharr lord could be was a public place. So the feelings built up inside Karne like steam in a boiler without a safety valve. Perhaps that was why Gharr lords were so often cruel or unreasonable: It was their only relief.

This time Karne's lid covered fear and fury. Fear that he came near to killing his closest friend. Fury at that friend doubting his courage. Egil did not know how Karne had held to the calm exterior as long as he had. Egil himself would have been near berserker rage in the same circumstances. The difference was, Egil would not have hidden it.

Karne's calm voice and face fell away and the harshness of the voice and face underneath made Karne seem much older than eighteen. "Now we're going to collect Richard and take him back to Breven to serve out his time. If we're lucky, there are no escort ships out here. If I'm lucky, you're right about Breven being the best revenge." Karne slid out of the door and onto the wing.

Egil took a deep, shaky breath, unclasped his safety belt, and stood slowly. His knees felt like water. "There has to have been a better way to stay out of sight," he muttered under his breath. "It'll be a very cold day in Hel before I let *him* fly again when he's feeling reckless. Gods!" Egil held out a hand. It was vibrating. He swore softly.

Karne stuck his head back inside the cabin. "You coming?" he snapped.

"In a minute. By all the gods, you could have killed us twenty times back there!"

" 'No man knows the time of his death, so why cower in a safe place.' " Karne turned away and jumped from the wing to the sand.

Egil bristled. One of his own favorite sayings, tossed back at him like that! And to have it quoted at him now!

Egil tossed emergency rations, a shelter, two reflectorized blankets, a knife, and a rope into his pack on top of the other equipment, stuck a beamer from the weapons rack under his belt, and joined Karne on the sandbar.

CHAPTER 15

Karne sprinted toward the bend that concealed Harlan and his flitter, hugging the bluff wall as he ran. Egil followed, his mind racing. With Karne in this reckless mood, what would he do? He had always been cool in battle, but now . . . ?

Karne crouched behind boulders on the riverbank and Egil crowded right up behind him. They looked around the boulders. Harlan and his pilot were attempting to repair the Kingsland flier. Apparently Karne's shot had damaged the engine as well as the wing. Three other men were picking up the last bits of camp equipment and refuse. In moments, there would be no evidence of the Harlan camp left for either satellite or fliers to see. Egil looked up at the sky and listened. He heard, faintly, the voices of Harlan and his pilot, but not even the faintest sound of the Council's fliers' engines. The smoke had cleared. Perhaps the Council fliers had not seen it.

Karne slipped partway around a boulder. He was within stunner distance of the Harlan men, but only just. Karne straightened, flattened himself against the boulder, and began easing himself toward a closer one. A warning went off in the back of Egil's brain. The dark blue Halarek uniform might help conceal Karne against the dark rocks, but there was something wrong out there. Something was missing. Several Kingsland men were missing. Metal brushed against

193

rock close above their heads. *Gods!* "Karne, watch out!"

Egil's warning came too late. A Kingsland soldier dropped from a low place on the bluff and slashed as Karne dodged sideways and spun to defend himself. In the moment before the second attacker reached Egil, Egil saw dark blood stream from Karne's shoulder and chest. Egil's opponent lunged for him, knife outstretched.

If he thought to kill me quietly, he needs better technique than he's got, Egil thought.

He knocked the man's knife away. His opponent immediately pulled his beamer. Egil needed both hands to stop him. He dropped his own weapon and gripped the soldier's wrist. The two of them spun, twisted, lurched back and forth. For a second, Egil caught a glimpse of Karne struggling to keep the knife away from himself. That tiny lapse of attention was all Egil's opponent needed. He twisted the beamer free and swung it toward Karne. *He's going to kill the Halarek first.* Egil knocked the beamer upward and out of the man's hand. Weaponless now, the Kingsland soldier lunged for Egil's throat. Egil met the lunge with a quick parry. He heard the thuds and scuffling behind him with painful clarity, but he could not spare a glance. Karne was much lighter than his opponent, weakened by blood loss and shock, and had never had Egil's hand-to-hand skills. Egil heard a soft gasp behind him that sent a chill up his spine. He ducked quickly under his opponent's guard, lunged up and sideways, and broke the man's back with a long-forbidden Drinn move.

Egil spun. Karne's opponent was sinking to the ground, an amazed look on his face, trying to push his intestines back inside his belly. Karne sagged against the bluff wall, as white as one of the Gharr could get. He, too, had a belly wound. Egil turned, grabbed his stunner from the ground, dialed it to "high stun," and sprayed the Kingsland flitter and the men around it. He watched only long enough to see Harlan fall with the rest, then cut away one of his sleeves with the Kingsland knife, made a pad of it for Karne to hold against the belly wound, and carried Karne to their flitter.

He laid Karne on the floor, folded a parka and stuck it under his head, raised his knees, and tied the pad on tightly with bandaging from the med-kit. The stream of blood seemed to have slowed a lot, but Karne still needed emergency medical help.

Harlan would come out of the effects of the stunner soon. Karne needed help now.

If Egil called Council, Harlan would get away and the Gharr would lose their freedom. Egil would lose his freedom. Karne would lose his life.

Karne might be bleeding to death inside right now.

Harlan would escape—

Egil dialed the emergency Council frequency, then set the flitter's crash alarm. That would broadcast a general emergency call and the flitter's location, and the broadcast should bring Council in a hurry. He looked again at Karne. He would have to hold on until Council came. If Harlan escaped, they both were lost.

Egil hooked the ship's supply of rope off the equipment rack and slid out onto the wing and then onto the ground. He sprinted back to the Kingsland flier. The men were stirring. He sprayed them again with the stunner, then tied them all, the soldiers in a cluster, Harlan in a portable package. He slung Harlan over his shoulder and hiked back to the flitter. Karne looked worse and there was no sign of Council. Egil remembered with bitterness how Karne had called and called for Council help and gotten nothing when he himself had lain in a guardpost at the edge of Zinn, his hands frozen.

Egil dumped Harlan into a seat and strapped him in, remembering his own extreme discomfort under similar conditions, thinking this was at least a small revenge. If Council didn't get here in seconds, he would take Karne home and hope he survived the trip. He certainly wouldn't survive if they stayed here.

Egil slid into the pilot's seat and examined the sky. Two Council-red fliers flashed over the nearest ridge, circled, landed upstream. Egil looked back at Karne. "Help's coming," he said gently. "Council heard us this time."

"They heard us at Post 105, too." Karne's voice was a thread of sound. "We couldn't hear them reply, that's all. By the time the med team arrived, you were gone." Karne closed his eyes and his chest rose and fell with rapid, shallow breaths.

Moments after the Council fliers landed, a soldier with the white circle of a medic on his shoulder was in the flitter, his forehead wrinkled in concern, his hands flashing here and there as he rebandaged the wound, injected Karne with something, motioned to Egil to help two more medics hold a litter level outside the passenger door. Another Council flier had landed while Egil was watching the medic. This one bore the white circle on wings and belly.

"The Lharr needs immediate help," the medic told Egil. "We're taking him to the nearest expert-care service, the clinic at Gildport. Follow us."

The medics had Karne on the litter and then in their flier in far less time than Egil would have thought possible. It was only as he watched the medical flier take off that Egil realized he had asked no questions, demanded no proof of identity, taken none of the similar safety precautions necessary on this world. It was too late to do anything about that now. He could only follow as the medic had told him to.

Egil took off after the med ship quickly. He heard Harlan's head bang into the sidewall, but did not look back. He commed Council as soon as he was up, told about Harlan's capture, and demanded a proper guard under the Gild's control to take Harlan back to Breven.

Harlan began to curse. Egil glanced over his shoulder for a fraction of a second. Harlan's face was red and looked as if it were swelling. Egil returned his eyes to the front. If he could read Rom, he could have set the autopilot, but he could not read Rom, so he must keep the Council flier in sight. Harlan swore steadily. Insults followed, insults on Egil and Karne and all their ancestors and descendants in thorough and scatological detail. He did all he could to prick Egil's honor hard enough to make him kill. What was insult to the Gharr was often not an insult to a Balderman, but enough of them stung. Quite enough of them. Egil kept repeating to himself that nine years in Breven would be far worse than death for Harlan. Far worse than death, far worse than death, he kept thinking, but repetition was not enough. Finally he turned and smiled at Harlan, making very sure his shadow would not hide that smile.

"My lord duke-designate," he said in gentle, polite tones, "I thought to take both your hands in return for the freezing of mine. But I agree with the Lharr. A far sweeter revenge will be to see you serve out the rest of your sentence. I hope to arrange to spend several more months on this gods-forsaken world, just to see House Harlan begin to fray around the edges and fall apart." It would not hurt to give Karne credit for the return-to-prison idea; the clan enmity was old and Harlan had had the upper hand for some years.

Harlan spat out a string of Rom insults that were beyond Egil's vocabulary, though he was quite sure they must have been the worst Harlan could think of at the moment.

"I've had enough of your voice for this trip, my lord."

The calm he felt, once he realized this really was the best revenge, surprised Egil. He pulled some tape from its storage compartment, whirled in his seat, grabbed the duke's chin, shoved his head back against the seat until his mouth had to stay closed, then taped his mouth shut. Harlan's dark eyes blazed. Egil looked into the rage in those eyes and smiled, grimly now. The Watchers had been right. Death would have been too easy for this one.

There was a hail from Konnor Holding. "Who goes there?" was the essence of the hail and it was usually answered automatically. Egil turned quickly back to the instruments and requested the coordinates to Gildport, just in case he lost sight of the faster Council ship. He jotted them down in his own world's language and felt immediate relief. No pilot likes to be aloft over strange country with neither landmarks nor com guidance. Harlan twisted and grunted and struggled against the rope. Egil ignored him.

In a short time, the narrow stone entrance shelters of the Gild were below. The Council flier's doors were open and med techs from the Gild had Karne out of the flitter and into the entrance shelter with great speed.

Egil hailed the port offices to request immediate permission to land and, minutes later, let the flitter down gently onto the landing pad. A prox-sensor opened the lift doors the moment Egil entered the entrance shelter and in moments more he was forty meters below the surface. The lift doors opened onto a large receiving room with the red rocket and gyro of the Gild painted large on the opposite wall. A man in a First Merchant's uniform came forward. Egil felt too drained to salute the First Merchant. The merchant did not seem to notice.

"You are the Lharr Halarek's off-world friend, Olafsson, of course. And Odin Olafsson's son. I understand your father has christened a new freighter in honor of your survival."

Egil could not help but smile, though it was a weak smile. With his size and coloring, he could be nothing but an off-worlder and, with the fuss the Gild made at World Council, almost everyone on Starker IV, and certainly every member of the Gild, knew of his connection to the merchant Odin Olafsson. It felt good, though, that his father would so honor him. Egil gave a great sigh and leaned against the nearest wall. All the starch seemed to have gone out of him.

"I'm Danielovitch," the First Merchant said. "The Lharr is in emergency surgery, of course. We'll let you know how he is as soon as we know. In the meantime, Grristen here will offer you what poor hospitality we have on such short notice." Danielovitch motioned a Gildclerk forward.

The clerk's short silver-gray fur and drooping features looked strange to Egil after seeing only Gharr and Watchers for so long.

"The doctors say it will be some time, sir." The XT's voice was as velvety as its fur. "Will you have a chair in the customs house, perhaps? Or would you rather sit in the park? The doctors will let you see the young lord as soon as that may be."

"The park." *I'm going to need some time to adjust to being back in "civilization," I think.* Prox-sensors, computers, XTs—all the trappings of life on Federation worlds, set here like an island in Starker IV's sea of feudalism and clan warfare.

The park was very small, but it had been carefully landscaped to seem larger than it was. It had a fountain at its center. Egil walked to the edge of the fountain, stepping only on the stones of the footpath so as not to touch the delicate, hothouse grass. The scent of the bluepines behind the fountain was a balm to his senses. The soft, even splashing of the fountain let his muscles loosen and his mind unwind. Harlan could stay where he was until Karne was taken care of. Egil would be taken care of, because he had kept his oath. The Watchers would have to keep theirs.

Egil lay carefully down on the grass and shut his eyes. It had been a very long day. It felt so good to lie flat and let his sore muscles go limp, to let his mind go limp. The steady sound of falling water was so very peaceful . . .

Someone was jostling his shoulder. "Sir? Sir?" It was the soft, furry voice of the XT customs steward. "House Halarek has commed and would like to speak with you. Perhaps you would like to see the young Lharr first? To reassure the Lady Kathryn?"

Egil nodded, his brain still too foggy to permit intelligible speech. He rolled over and stood slowly. He shook his head to rid himself of the last of the cobwebs. "Is the Lharr going to be all right?"

"The doctors think so. He's just come out of surgery, so he's not awake yet, but you can look in on him. The doctors say it could have been much worse."

They now stood on one of the narrow streets that bordered the park. The XT looked up at Egil. "The pad police report a bound man in your flitter, sir. The duke-designate in Harlan, sir."

Egil needed a moment to remember. "Oh, yes. He's an escaped Council prisoner on his way back to Council. The Lharr was hurt during his capture."

The XT nodded. "Then I will tell the police all is as it should be." He led the way down a bright street toward the infirmary.

Egil watched his back for a second, then followed. *Either he/it doesn't know how important our prisoner is or he/it just isn't letting on.* That thought was followed quickly by another. *What would the Gild do when it learned he was keeping Harlan in his flitter like a sack of potatoes?*

Egil was soon to find out. The Gild's First Merchant met him outside Karne's door and waited until he had satisfied himself that his friend was truly still alive and breathing, though deeply unconscious. When Egil came out of the room again, the First Merchant took him politely by the elbow and steered him to a nearby office that was tastefully decorated in quiet pastels and sparse furniture.

"The psychologist's office, sir," the First Merchant explained. "I've just learned that you have the duke-designate in Harlan prisoner and I need to know your intentions toward him."

Egil looked the merchant up and down carefully, trying to judge what the man was thinking. "Harlan is on his way back to prison at Breven, from which he escaped some weeks ago, as I'm sure you've heard."

"Breven is halfway across the planet, sir."

"I'm aware of that, gentlehom. We intended to take him to Ontar to await Council pickup."

The merchant's lips pursed. "As you assuredly know, young sir, the Gild lives on its neutrality. Gild Central and I hesitate to allow the duke-designate to leave our territory in the hands of his clan enemy. What if something untoward should happen to him between here and Council pickup?"

"You question the honor of Halarek?"

The First Merchant gave him a you-of-all-people-should-know look. "House Halarek is no different from the others of the Nine, sir."

Egil began to see the merchant's point, although he did not like it. The Gild *would* be implicated if something "untoward" happened to the Heir in Harlan. He felt as if he had to stand up for his friend, anyway. "Karne Halarek is nothing like his sire."

"Be that as it may, the young Lharr will not be ruling his House for the next month or two. When would the Council come for this man?"

"Council meds led me here and I commed Council on the way. When a proper escort comes for Harlan, he's Council's. Though I don't trust Gormsby's Council," Egil added under his breath.

The First Merchant hesitated a moment, then spoke. "We heard that call, young sir. The district officer for Council in this area is a man of the previous chairman's. Gormsby's. The flitter's crash alarm automatically identified it as Halarek. The officer will send no fliers to help Halarek take the duke-designate back to prison. Medical help he can't deny without losing his job."

Egil swore—briefly, feelingly, and in the saga-language, so as not to offend the First Merchant. Then he looked intently at the Gildsman. "Would the Gild be willing to take on the burden of the duke-designate, perhaps to deliver him in person to Chairman Gashen?"

The Gildman's features sharpened. "What would be the Gild's benefit in that?"

Egil almost laughed. How like a merchant. "Why, a continued unsullied reputation for neutrality, even in clan feuds, gentlehom. Think of the distressing possibilities if he left your hands and suffered some unhappy accident."

It looked for a moment as if that would not be enough to convince the merchant. Egil thought it was a very good plan. It would take the Harlan Heir off his hands. He did not like the idea of being responsible for the man. There were still assassins looking for him; there was the danger of having him in Ontar, however well guarded the manor house was. There had already been com leaks, Karne's pet uhl-uhl had been tortured and murdered there, and Karne himself had almost been assassinated there by an officer he had decommissioned. No, the duke and his troubles were far better left in Gild and Council hands. Any Harlan loyalists in Council would hesitate a long time before they angered the Gild by killing someone under Gild protection and the Gild would find some way to make its hand in the matter an addition to its reputation for neutrality and fair play.

In the end, the Gildsman agreed to take Harlan and turn him over to the Council. Egil felt like shouting his relief, but he instead bowed decorously and delayed his shout until he was with Karne in Karne's closed room. Karne put limp, pale hands over his ears, far too slowly to protect them. Egil gripped his friend's shoulders with strong, gentle fingers.

"You're going to heal okay. I'm already healed and free of the Runners. Harlan's on his way back to prison. What more could we ask?"

Karne looked up at his large, loud friend with a faint smile on his tired face. "A little piece and quiet," he said.